Song
of the
Hummingbird

Graciela Limón

Arte Público Press
Houston, Texas
1996

This volume is made possible through grants from the National Endowment for the Arts (a federal agency) and the Andrew W. Mellon Foundation.

Recovering the past, creating the future

Arte Público Press
University of Houston
Houston, Texas 77204-2090

Cover illustration and design by Kath Christensen

Limón, Graciela.
    Song of the hummingbird / by Graciela Limón.
        p.   cm.
    ISBN 1-55885-157-7 (cloth: alk. paper)
    ISBN 1-55885-091-0 (pbk: alk. paper)
    1. Indians of Mexico—First contact with Europeans—Fiction. 2. Aztecs—First contact with Europeans—Fiction. 3. Mexico—History—Conquest, 1519–1540—Fiction. 4. Indian women—Mexico—Fiction. I. Title.
PS3562.I464S66   1996
813'.54—dc20   95-37666
                                   CIP

"Go to the region of the wild maguey to erect a dwelling
        of cactus and maguey,
        and there place woven mats.

"You will then go to where light begins,
        and there you must scatter your flowers.

"You will then go to where death abides,
        in that land of white flowers you must also
        scatter your flowers.

"And then you will go to the land sown with seed,
        there you must also cast your flowers.

"And then you will go to the region of thorns,
        and in the land of thorns you also must
        scatter your flowers.

"And you will scatter your flowers, and thus
        reach the gods."

> *Words of Coatlicuie,*
>   *Goddess of the Earth and Death*
>   *Mother of Quetzalcoatl and Huitzilopochtli*

It is a pleasure to acknowledge and thank Dr. Nicolás Kanellos, publisher of Arte Público Press, and his staff. I also extend my gratitude to him for editing this work. *Song of the Hummingbird* is my third novel published by Arte Público Press and I say at this point that I consider it a privilege to be part of its team of many outstanding U.S. Latina and Latino authors. I also thank Sister Martin Byrne, colleague and friend, who read the manuscript and shared her valuable insights.

G.L.

Author's Note

The protagonist of this novel says to Father Benito Lara, "My name is Huitzitzilin, but because I know the difficulty my language causes your tongue, you may call me Hummingbird, since that is what the word means."

I'm grateful for the protagonist's thoughtfulness. Nonetheless, I have chosen to use her name as it is in her native Nahuatl. I want her to know that my respect for her begins with the recognition of her name as it was given to her at birth. Although the name is initially difficult to pronounce, I know that my readers will soon join me in admiring its beauty and resonance.

Huitzitzilin also uses the word Mexica when speaking of her people even though most of us have come to use the word Aztec in its place. Here also, my readers will find me following her example.

The protagonist of *Song of the Hummingbird* will tell her own story. However, let me first say something about her life, her times and the events that she witnessed. Of noble Mexica birth, she was a young woman when the Spaniards arrived in Mexico, at that time known as Tenochtitlan. Like most of her people, she experienced the awe caused by those bearded white men when they first arrived; a wonderment that soon gave way to the outrage of seeing the devastation of her land, the disruption of her life, and the end of civilization as she knew it.

Huitzitzilin not only witnessed the obliteration of Tenochtitlan, leaving hardly a vestige of its greatness, but she suffered the loss of her Mexica identity. Along with her people, she experienced being forced to discard her traditional dress and to take up strange garments; to change her name; to speak a language foreign to her tongue; to forsake her ancestral gods; and in the end, to be part of the diaspora of a once great civilization.

I now ask my readers to listen carefully to her tale—her song—which is a version of those times different from what has been affirmed for centuries. Her story is told from the point of view of an indigenous woman. It is one which will at first appear reversed, like the reflection of writing in a mirror; but it is Huitzitzilin's story. It is believable because she was a participant and a witness. Like that same reflection in the mirror now grown dim with the passage of years, her story is what happened, even though not recorded in the history written by the conquerors of her land.

G.L.

Song
of the
Hummingbird

Chapter I

Coyoacán—the outskirts of Tenochtitlan-Mexico—1583.

The Franciscan monk approached the convent entrance, cautiously tugged at the rope that rang the bell, and waited tensely until he heard the shuffling steps of the gatekeeper. When a small window cut into the door opened, he caught a glimpse of a woman's wrinkled face. The white wimple framing her head hid any other signs of age.

"Good morning, Sister. I'm the new confessor, Father Benito Lara."

The nun had small, myopic eyes that stared at the priest's face unabashedly "You're young. Much younger than the one we had before you."

She shut the panel with a thud that forced him to blink involuntarily, then he heard the brass key turn loudly in the lock, followed by the creaking of hinges as the door lumbered open. Father Benito stepped into the vast cloister enclosed within the convent. He was momentarily halted by the nun who took time to scan him from top to bottom. She saw that he was of a medium build, thin, light-complected, and that his hair, already beginning to thin to baldness, was chestnut-colored. The rough, brown wool of the habit he wore was as yet not frayed or threadbare.

"I see that you haven't been a friar that long. Let us see how this land treats you and if you can accustom yourself to it."

Father Benito did not catch the full meaning of the nun's words, but he nevertheless followed her quietly when she motioned him to come into the corridor. To his left, the priest took in the images of saints, prophets and angels sculpted into the walls. To his right, his eyes scanned a garden shaded by orange, lemon and pomegranate trees. The place was lined with clay pots filled with geranium and bougainvillea flowers. A large stone fountain was at the center of the garden. As he walked, he could make out the sound of splashing water, its tinkling mingled with the scraping of his sandals on the tile floor. He followed silently until the nun led him to a secluded nook at the end of the main cloister, where he was able to make out the figure of an elderly woman. He saw that she was sitting in the center of a patch of pale sunlight.

"She's been nagging Mother Superior to get her a confessor. Really, she can be such a nuisance even though she is an old woman! She knew that we had to wait until a new priest was assigned to the convent, but oh, no! She demanded special attention right away! She keeps reminding us that she's *nooo-bi-li-ty*." The nun puckered her mouth and mockingly slurred the word.

"Please, Sister, it's no bother. Besides, as you say, she is very old, and perhaps she senses that her end is near. The spirit many times tells the body..."

The nun did not allow Father Benito to finish. "These people are not like us, Father. They have no spirit!"

Even though she had mumbled, the priest made out what she said.

"Don't say that, Sister. You're wrong. We're all God's children. Now, if you will allow us to be alone for a while. I'll let you know when I'm finished."

When the priest was alone, he stood for a long while gazing at the frail woman with the waning autumn light spilling over her bony shoulders. She appeared to be lost in thought and seemed to sing as she rocked back and forth in her chair. He realized that she was even older than he had thought when he first saw her. Her skin looked brittle and transparent, yellowish-brown in tone. His eyes shifted to concentrate on the old woman's hands and noticed that they were tiny and tightly encased in thin skin; they fluttered nervously from time to time.

"Like brown swallows," he thought.

He stepped closer, hoping to get her attention, but she was oblivious to his presence. As he got closer to her, he confirmed that he had been right. She was singing, but he could not make out the words of her song. Father Benito was now so near the old woman that he could see that her face was small, skeletal, and that one of her eye sockets was empty; its darkened hollow was marked

11

with scars. Her hair was white, coarse and stringy, and it was fastened tightly at the nape of her neck.

The priest was gaping at the old woman with such concentration that when her face suddenly whipped around to look at him, he was startled. He flinched with unexpected fright. Her good eye, he saw, was bird-like and it glared at him with a black, flinty pupil that made him shiver.

"Ah! You must be the priest who has come to hear my last confession."

Father Benito was taken by surprise and he couldn't find words with which to answer. As he was scolding himself for being so awkward, he heard himself say, "Last confession? Señora, what makes you think such a thing?"

She giggled, exposing toothless gums. Her nose hooked downward, giving her the look of an eagle. "Perhaps I should say, my *only* confession, because I have never told any of your priests the real sins of my life. Come, sit here by me."

She pointed to a small chair that Father Benito had not seen before. He moved closer to her as he tried to make himself comfortable in the seat. She stared at him steadily, making him squirm and fidget with one of the thick knots on the cord that hung from his waist. Not knowing what to say, the priest mutely reached into his pocket and pulled out a purple stole. The woman looked at him with more intensity as he clumsily fixed the strip of cloth around his shoulders.

"You're very young. Where were you born?"

"In Carmona, Señora," he stammered.

"Over there?" She pointed her nose at a spot somewhere behind him. He unthinkingly swiveled his head to look at where she had pointed, but saw only the faded stucco of the convent wall. After a few moments, however, he understood what she had asked.

"Yes, I'm from Spain. I was born in a small village outside of Seville." He paused for a few seconds, waiting for her to speak, but she had returned to her silence. Clearing his voice, Father Benito asked, "And you, Señora, where were you born?"

"Here."

With that, the woman returned to her silence.

Father Benito again cleared his throat. "Shall we begin?"

She ignored his question. "I was born here, where this building, this house of women has now been constructed. My father's house was built on this very place."

Seeing that the priest was confused by what she had said, she added more. "That house—the first one—was destroyed by Captain General Cortés before he gave the land to your people. He and his captains did much of that, but I suppose it was all meant to be."

The woman focused her eye on the monk. "How old are you?"

"Twenty-seven."

She ran her tongue over dry lips as she wagged her head in calculation. I was born eighty-two years ago, during the Melancholy Days. In your reckoning, spring of the year 1501. What I am remembering happened many years before you were born. But perhaps you know some of the details of those times. I mean those days when your captains and your four-legged beasts came across the waters to infest our world."

Father Benito was jolted by the sharp edge of her remark, and for an instant he felt like retorting with his own ideas, reminding her of the blessings the Spaniards had brought to her people. He decided instead to keep his words to himself. After all, he told himself, she was only an old woman and they had just met.

The woman sighed, moving her head from side to side despondently. "We were guided by a divine trinity. One brother was all-knowing, the other was a preacher and priest, but the last one thirsted for human hearts."

"You're confused, Señora. That is not the Trinity at all."

Father Benito's voice was urgent, rising above the soft garden sounds; it echoed in the hollows of the cloister ceilings.

She ignored the monk and spoke as if lost in the solitude of another time, another place. "With the passage of time my people grew to revere this third brother, forgetting the good one, listening to words prompting the Mexicas to wage war in this land and to gather new offerings for him, the lord of blood. So it was that my people abandoned the planting of maize and became a nation of tiger and eagle warriors."

Father Benito's body shivered with the same revulsion he used to feel when he was a schoolboy listening to his teachers tell of what the explorers had encountered in the Indies. He remembered letters, circulated and read everywhere, even from church pulpits. He recalled vivid descriptions of bloodied temples, hearts carved out by obsidian knives, human flesh devoured by blood-encrusted warlocks who called themselves priests. His mind flashed back to the solemn requiem mass that had been dedicated to the memory of two soldiers, natives of his hometown; they had been slashed and eaten by those sorcerers. He was deep into his memories when he was startled back to the present by the woman's words.

"In the beginning, I didn't understand why the tribes surrounding us became our enemies so easily, but now that I am old, it's clear to me. It was because of that god's constant demand for human hearts that we became feared, and then detested. It had to be! Then, on top of it all, the preacher god unleashed his wrath on our faithlessness—just as he had promised. It was at that time that your people came to devastate us."

Father Benito knew that this was not a confession, but he was intrigued by what the woman was saying. He had never heard of those events told by someone like her, someone native to that land. He moved closer to her, straining to grasp her lilting words, which had become more and more accented as she drifted back in time.

"The Mexica people were splintered by the Spaniards and we were cast out of our kingdom like scattered leaves. We had thought that we were the light of the universe and that our city was the mirror of the world. Instead we were uprooted and destroyed by your people. When it first happened, we were wracked by hunger and pestilence; all we did was weep because we saw that now we were the strangers in this land, not you. Our warriors were humiliated and died with dirt in their mouths. As for me, I was young then, and with my children I walked aimlessly among crowds of lost, drifting people. Like everyone else, I wailed, hoping that the gods would feel pity."

She stopped abruptly as if realizing that she had revealed secrets unintentionally. After some moments she sighed, and whispered, "But that was then. It's over now."

Father Benito felt embarrassed by what he had heard. Not knowing what to say, he waited, hoping that the right words would come to him. Nothing else occurred to him, so he decided to have the woman begin her confession.

"Señora, the morning is drawing to a close, and I must return to say mass this afternoon. Please, shall we begin? In name of the Father, and of the Son, and of the Holy Gh..."

She interrupted the priest. "You want to hear my sins, don't you?" Her voice was shrill and transformed from its previous soft tones. When Father Benito stared at her without answering, she added, "You don't even know my name, and you want to hear my sins."

"It is you who have called me to come. Please! Let us begin." This time he silently made the sign of the cross.

"My name is Huitzitzilin, but because I know the difficulty my language causes your tongue, you may call me Hummingbird, since that is what the word means." She smoothed the folds of the shawl that outlined the sharp angles of her shoulders.

"Although I am now destitute, I am of noble birth, a descendent of Mexica kings. My life has been a path which has taken unforeseen turns. The first of those unexpected twists happened long before the arrival of your captains, when I was still a girl. On that day Zintle and I went swimming."

"Swimming is not a sin."

"Is fornication a sin?"

Father Benito blushed so intensely that the skin around his eyebrows took on a purplish hue. He was again without words, so he averted his face from her questioning gaze.

"Zintle was my cousin. He, too, was noble and like me, he paid a high price for that happenstance. You'll hear more about him later on. On the day I am speaking of, he and I ran toward the river. We romped and jumped. We skipped and lunged. We ran in a straight path, then we snaked back and forth, all the while letting out whoops and squeals of joy. We ran, unconscious of our young vigor, taking the gift of energy lightly. We ran until we lost our breath. Then we flopped on the watercress that covered the river embankment. I can still smell its sweetness, its damp, green matting."

Huitzitzilin stopped speaking and turned to look at the monk. She saw that even though his head was lowered, he seemed to be listening to her.

"We laughed, snorting through our noses and then giggling even more at the sounds we were making. What made us laugh so much? I don't know."

"Señora, forgive me, but this is really not..."

Huitzitzilin held up her hand stiffly, sticking it in front of the monk's face as she countered his complaint. "It's coming!"

"What?"

"The sin. That's what you want to hear, isn't it?"

This time Father Benito's face reflected irritation, but he kept it to himself.

"It was Zintle's idea. He said that we should take off our clothes. I did. When I looked at him I saw that we were different. At the time, I had not yet reached my first bleeding."

The woman stopped speaking and looked at Father Benito. He was self-consciously staring at the tiled floor, so she returned to her confession.

"We jumped into the water, splashing each other, screaming shrilly, as if the drops burned our skin. We pretended fear when one would push the other into the water, and we scooped gulps of water into our mouths, spitting it out, spraying each other.

"Then Zintle did something that both of us thought very funny. He waded out to the edge, plucked a large green leaf from an overhanging tree, poked a hole through its center with his finger, and then hooked the leaf onto his penis. We were both astounded that the leaf looked exactly like a green and gold stemmed flower clinging to his body. At first we stared at it, then we burst out laughing. Then he dared me to do the same thing, but all I could do was stick my finger through a leaf and hold it tightly to my body.

"When we tired of so much laughing, we left the water to lie on the grass to dry ourselves. Without saying anything, Zintle rolled over onto his side, his face just above mine. We had never done this before, and even though we knew that it was wrong for a maiden to do such a thing before marriage, we did nothing to stop it. There was something different in his eyes, and I think he saw the same look in my eyes. Soon I felt his breath on my cheeks and his lips brushing my eyes, my chin, my lips. Then he got on top of me and I could feel his masculine part hovering in the area between my legs."

"Señora, please! You can be sure that I understand clearly that you fornicated with that boy. You need not describe it any further." Father Benito got to his feet and stood in front of Huitzitzilin. He looked down at her uplifted face; his eyes were stern. "Besides, I cannot believe that you have not confessed this sin before. A woman of your age..."

"No! I have never said this to anyone because I have never told anyone about my life."

The priest seemed perplexed. "Why are you telling me these things?"

"Because I will soon die, and someone must know how it was that I and my people came to what we are now. Please, young priest, sit here and listen to me."

Father Benito obeyed her despite his evident desire to leave. "I absolve you of your sins." With one hand held flat against his chest he lifted the other in preparation to utter the prayer of absolution.

But Huitzitzilin interrupted him. She spoke rapidly. "Wait a minute! There's more."

"There's more?"

The priest, hand frozen in midair, quizzically echoed the woman's words. He gaped at the woman for a long time before he realized that his mouth was hanging open. Knowing that he looked foolish, he clamped it shut; the clashing sound caused by his teeth startled him. He looked down at his feet for some time before he decided what to do.

"I must leave now. I'll return tomorrow at this time."

Chapter II

Early next morning, Father Benito walked hurriedly, slipping now and then on the rough cobblestones as he made his way to the convent. He was still thinking of the old woman who was waiting for him in the dark cloister. He absentmindedly shook his head, realizing that he had been unable to forget her or her words, even while saying mass or eating with his brother friars. She had fascinated him, and he wanted to know more about her because she was different from what his teachers in Spain had taught him about the natives of this land.

He muttered under his breath, asking himself why it had not occurred to him before that the people of this new mission might be like his own people. The old woman had unexpectedly injected this thought into his mind, and the newness of it made him uncomfortable. She had even spoken of a father, a home, a family. The writings and instructions given him in preparation for his work of evangelization had not spoken of such things, and he chided himself for his ignorance.

Huitzitzilin had confessed a sin of the flesh, something that had happened even to him when he was a boy. This transgression of her youth captivated him; it told him that she was like him, and like everyone else. More important, as with his own people, she admitted that the act was wrong, and that she had known that it was wrong. How, Benito asked himself, did she understand that it was evil at a time when she was not yet a Christian? As he stopped at the entrance to the convent, he paused momentarily, wondering what other sins the woman had to confess.

Father Benito yanked at the cord and the bell clanged noisily. He heard shuffling steps come near and pause, and then the peep door swung open. The same tiny eyes of the day before peered out at him, and then the entrance creaked open without the gatekeeper saying anything. The priest stepped over the threshold; he, too, kept silent while the nun led him to the far end of the cloister. This time the monk was looking for the old woman, not bothering to notice the garden or its surroundings.

"Buenos días, Señora."

The priest stood at a distance from Huitzitzilin, and he wondered if she had moved since he last saw her, because she was seated in the same place and she was wearing the same clothing. As on the day before, she was humming and rocking in the chair. Several minutes passed before she turned to Father Benito, lifted her frail arm and beckoned him to take his place next to her.

"Young priest, I have a sin to confess to you today, but first, may I tell you more about me and the ways that used to be mine?"

He sat next to her without speaking. He wanted to know more about her people, but he feared that she would misunderstand his interest as approval of the unholy deeds they had performed in the name of religion.

"Señora," Benito spoke slowly, "you must forget the past beliefs and practices of your people; they are gone, never to return. More especially, those ways belonged to the devil; they were filled with sin. I think that we should instead continue your confession."

Huitzitzilin stared at Father Benito as he withdrew the stole from the side pocket of his habit and placed it around his shoulders. Her look was filled not with defiance but with bewilderment. After a few moments, however, she looked away and gazed down at her lap where her hands twitched. She began to hum quietly until the priest shifted uncomfortably in his seat.

"Our gods were capricious."

"Please, don't utter such words."

"Why not?"

"Because it is idolatry to worship stone images as your people did in the past."

"Your temples are filled with statues!"

Huitzitzilin's voice was sharp and her words put Father Benito on the defensive. He glared at her silently, hesitating to answer because he was torn. On the one hand, his recent preparation to evangelize these parts had indoctrinated him to respond to such an accusation; it was not a new one. On the other hand, the old woman had uttered her thoughts with such conviction and intel-

ligence that he felt himself unsure and nearly agreed
with her.

He mulled this over for a few moments, then sighed
deeply as he nodded in affirmation. Nonetheless, he
made the sign of the cross just as if he were preparing to
hear a confession. In the meantime an idea was beginning to take shape in his mind. He told himself that
what this woman had to say about her people might be
as valuable as what the captains of the first discovery
had written and dispatched to Spain. He might even
gather enough information from her to compile a work
that could be of use to those following him.

"By all means, Señora, let me hear about your
ways."

"Of my childhood, my sixth year stands out as one of
the most memorable because, you see, it was the year in
which the Mexicas observed the Hill of the Star, a ceremony that came only once every fifty-two years, a time
when a period ended, giving way to a new one. A new era
was not guaranteed, however; it depended solely on the
whim of the gods, and knowing this made everyone ner-
vous.

"We were in the time of the fifth sun and we had up
to then been able to retain the favor of the gods. But previous races had not been so fortunate, and they had been
destroyed either by being devoured by wildcats or by
being transformed into monkeys. There were also floods
and famines that destroyed others."

Father Benito was listening intently, but he soon
realized that this was not new information. He had read
several chronicles written by missionaries and captains

that told of how the Mexicas reckoned time. He had also studied the material as a university student, and he suddenly felt his head ache just as it had when he used to try to pronounce the consonant-riddled language of these people.

As Huitzitzilin spoke, he remembered the days when he was forced to sit through tedious, detailed instructions by teachers who had recently returned from the Indies. Each one gave a different version of Mexica rituals, names and practices.

The monk was nevertheless curious, and wanted to know if the woman had something new to tell him. "Why was this moment so important to you if you were just a child?"

"That time was important for me because of three reasons. The first was that Zintle, a child like me, was there, too."

"The same boy you spoke of yesterday?"

"Yes. The same one; he was the one I loved. The second reason was that I saw for the first time, very closely, our king. You know his name. Moctezuma. And the final reason was that, as it turned out, that ceremony was indeed the last; one destined to mark the extinction of our world. Our era did come to an end after all. Oh, we were not destroyed by floods, or eaten by tigers. Instead, your people came and devoured us."

Father Benito's head whipped around to glare at the woman, and he knew that his eyes reflected the offense he was feeling. But Huitzitzilin's face was turned away from him. She seem transfixed, as if her spirit were elsewhere. He allowed a few minutes to pass, hoping to regain control of his emotions, and as he did this, he struggled to understand her way of thinking. When he finally spoke, he was glad to hear that his voice was serene and not angry.

"We have not devoured your people. Instead, we have brought our Savior's redemption."

"Yes, yes! I've heard all about it," Huitzitzilin interrupted Father Benito abruptly. Her voice again had an edge. "On that night, Moctezuma led his entourage to the place of honor. I still remember him and the dignity with which he carried his head, his body, his entire being. The color of his skin was mahogany. His face was oval-shaped, his forehead was wide, and his eyes blazed like those of the jaguar. His garments on that occasion were of black cotton, even the quetzal feathers in his headdress had been dyed black. His jewelry was all gold because he was both king and priest."

Father Benito realized that he was hearing a description that no chronicle or letter had ever conveyed. With the exception of Captain Hernán Cortés and the few men who had survived the battles for this city, no one had lived to tell of the emperor. Even now, most Spaniards thought him nothing more than a legend. But Huitzitzilin's remark about the king's priesthood rankled Benito, so he put his hand on her shoulder and pressed it softly.

"You don't mean that the king was a priest, do you? Perhaps he was a magician or something similar because, be assured, he could not have been a priest."

"He was a priest! And, as you say in your own mass, a priest is a priest forever."

Father Benito sighed, and kept quiet only because he wanted to hear more.

"Moctezuma stood by the High Priest and together they began the prayer to our gods. Both men raised their arms in reverence, the fingers of their hands taut and crisped so that in the gloom of that night of nights, they appeared like the claws of black-plumed birds carved in stone."

Huitzitzilin turned to face Father Benito. "Do you want to hear their prayer, young priest? Or will you be chastised by those above you for listening to me?"

He hadn't realized that she knew so much about his way of life and his congregation, one which strictly forbade even a reference to the practices the Church was trying to eradicate. But Father Benito wanted to know, and he shifted in the chair as he felt a new surge of curiosity overcome him. He nervously looked over his shoulder as if to assure himself that no one was overhearing what the old woman was about to say.

"Yes. I want to hear." His voice was barely a whisper.

"Moctezuma and the High Priest chanted together like this. 'O lord of the feathered left hand! O lord sorcerer bird...'"

"Stop! Stop!" Father Benito suddenly regretted having allowed the woman to repeat the satanic stanzas in his presence. "Please don't say any more! You should try to forget those unholy words."

"Why?"

"Because they conjure the devil himself out of his pit. Don't you see? You have ears, don't you? You heard that the prayer calls upon the lord of sorcery; that is Satan himself!"

"Perhaps."

The priest thought that he heard her giggle softly, and he felt embarrassed. Maybe, he thought, he had been exaggerated in his response to the incantation which might have been a brief introduction to more interesting details. He tried another approach.

"Señora, why don't you tell me about what happened that night? You can, of course, omit the prayers."

Huitzitzilin smiled. "Yes, I can tell you much about that night. Remember that it was the most important in our history because, as it now turns out, it was the end of our fifth sun.

"Let me tell you of what the High Priest did. He began with an incantation—I won't repeat the words—with a voice that seemed to boom from the bottom of the giant drum. His chanting called upon gods of whom I had never before heard. He shook the sacred rattle with his right hand and slashed at the black night air with the obsidian knife which he grasped in his left hand. The raven-colored garments that covered his body fluttered as he gyrated round and round. Then he began, sinuously, like a snake, to undulate up and down as if coupling with a woman. He did this over and again as his waist-long hair, tangled and encrusted with the blood of immolation, flapped in the wind."

When Huitzitzilin paused, she looked over to Father Benito, who sat stiffly with his face buried in his hands. He was hunched over and said nothing for a long time, but she knew that he had heard her words and that he was in turmoil.

"I will tell you no more about this because I see that you are distressed at the mention of copulation and blood. Are these, however, not the ways of all men? The Mexicas were not the only ones to defile and sacrifice the enemy. But, enough! I will end by telling you that the star we awaited that night did indeed appear. But to no avail, because even with its appearance, as I have already told you, our era came to an end."

Father Benito looked at Huitzitzilin, and his eyes betrayed the agitation that was tormenting him. He was torn by repulsion and fear, as well as by an inexplicable desire to know more about the old woman and her past. However, he knew that he had transgressed the boundaries of a mere search for knowledge and information when he willingly listened to what was forbidden by his own religion. He felt bitterly culpable because it was he who had encouraged her to invoke that sordid past.

Huitzitzilin sensed Father Benito's anguish and she decided to turn to the reason he was there, her confession. "Let me now confess another of my sins, young priest. I remained here in my father's house until the age of fifteen. Shortly after that time, I was sent to Tenochtitlan to complete my preparation for marriage. There, I became part of the court that surrounded Moctezuma, thereby exposing myself to partners that might have been eligible for matrimony with me."

Father Benito began to regain his composure as the woman spoke of practices that sounded almost the same as those of his own people, and he gratefully prepared himself to hear her confession. This time he was patient, waiting for her to get to the sin that would end his afternoon visit.

"Zintle was also sent to the court because, as I have told you, he was related by blood to Moctezuma and thereby had to be trained in case he might one day be eligible for governor, or even king."

"And you fornicated again!"

The priest's voice was smug, bordering on sarcastic. However, it was relief that he was feeling because here at least was a sin with which he could deal. Weakness of the flesh was well known to Holy Mother Church, unlike the demonic ways of the woman's people.

Huitzitzilin looked at the priest; her stare was a mix of offense as well as hostility, as if she had been robbed or cheated out of her words.

"Yes, many times over. He and I took every opportunity to love one another. Until the month when my bleeding stopped and I knew that I was with child. At that time I went to the healer, a woman not too much older than I, but one who knew the secrets of herbs. She prepared a substance and put it in a pot which she cooked. Then I sat on the pot so that the fumes it gave off entered my body. Next day, I was rid of the child that would have had me killed before my time."

Father Benito was stunned by Huitzitzilin's admission. First he gawked at her, not knowing what to say, then he looked down, staring at the leather straps of his sandals. His mind groped and floundered in an attempt to find pardon for what she had done. This was far greater, he acknowledged, than a mere sin of the flesh.

"You took the life of an unborn child, and you are asking for forgiveness?"

"Who is it who forgives? You or your god."

"God. I am only his instrument."

"Well, then, you must absolve me."

"Only if you are repentant."

"I would have been killed if he had discovered it."

"He? Do you mean that boy with whom…"

"No! Not him. I mean the man to whom I was at the time betrothed. His name was Tetla, and I had been given to him as a concubine. It was as if I were to be his wife. He would have had my heart cut out for deceiving him with another man. So you see, it was the life of the unborn child, or mine. What would you have done in my place?"

The priest was appalled by her question. "It's impossible to put myself in your place. I'm a man, not a woman."

"Then don't judge me."

"I'm not judging you. I'm merely asking if you repent of your most grievous sin."

"I would do it again because it meant my life."

Benito was exhausted by the rapid, almost hostile exchange of words. He was shocked by the woman's determination and by her boldness.

"I want to absolve you, but you must give me time."

"Yes. I want you to return because there is much more that I have to confess."

When the monk stepped out into the early evening, his head ached and his empty stomach growled. As he walked toward the monastery, he wondered why it was

31

that his path had steered him to the door of such a woman. He was intrigued as well as confused because he had not imagined that the natives of this land could be so complex. Above all, he was astounded at being repelled yet attracted by her.

Chapter III

"Priest, I have often heard your brother monks say
that it is a sin for a woman to deceive her husband
about her virginity before they are married. Do you
think this way?"

"Yes."

Father Benito had returned to be with Huitzitzilin.
The previous night had been difficult for him because he
had been unable to sleep, thinking of her. She had confessed to the willful killing of her unborn child, and he
knew that as a priest he was obliged to absolve her. Yet
he was in conflict because he couldn't find forgiveness
for her. On the other hand, her argument that she had
feared for her life was something that he turned over in
his mind, and finally he began to appreciate her circumstances.

After morning mass, Benito spoke to Father Anselmo, the prior, hoping to find guidance regarding the
Indian woman's revelations and their unexpected,
abrupt tangents. Their conference lasted more than two
hours, and after that Father Benito felt at peace, now
understanding that what he was to do was to discern the

separation between Huitzitzilin's sins and the customs of her people. The first he was to absolve and forget; the second he was to commit to paper.

Trying to deflect her impending confession, Benito prompted her in another direction. "Please tell me what you remember of this city during your youth."

"Tenochtitlan was a city of unimaginable grandeur and elegance," she responded. "It was a jewel and its setting was Anahuac, a valley flanked by volcanoes, mountains and fertile land. Our city was built on an island in the center of a lake. It's palaces, temples and marketplaces were of a beauty you cannot conceive."

Huitzitzilin interrupted the description and looked at Benito, a coy smile on her lips. "Shall I tell you more about Zintle and me?"

Father Benito's eyes snapped away from Huitzitzilin's face, trying to conceal the surge of blood that colored his cheeks and forehead. Inwardly, he reproached himself for betraying squeamishness as she alluded to her sexual transgressions. Again hoping to distract the woman, he asked, "May I, from time to time, write what you say?"

"I thought you were to forget the sins uttered in confession."

"Oh, you're right. However, it's not your sins that I would put on paper. Rather, it would be the many interesting things you say regarding your people."

Father Benito reached for a leather bag he had placed at his feet. From it he withdrew sheets of paper and a small ink pot. Then he fumbled for several moments, struggling to find the quill he thought he had brought along with the paper. He finally located it and returned his attention to Huitzitzilin, who seemed amused and entertained by his floundering. She put aside speaking more of Zintle.

"When I arrived in Tenochtitlan, I was housed with Ahuitzotl, my grandfather. It was there that I was to await Tetla's proposal for me to become one of his concubines. I must confess that my heart, though young, was a deep well of turmoil during those months. My spirit was confused, and it was torn by the emotions that have stalked me like sinister shadows ever since then. I was anguished by fear of what I knew would be Tetla's response to being cheated of my virginity.

Father Benito nervously interrupted her. "May I ask you to first tell me of the traditions regarding marriages and leave your confession to the end?"

"Very well. But the mention of my loss of virginity is not meant to be a confession, young priest."

The monk cleared his voice but said nothing. Instead he adjusted the paper on his lap and dipped the quill into the ink pot. He looked at Huitzitzilin, letting her know that he was ready to begin recording her words.

"It was morning when I was summoned to hear Tetla's messenger repeat the plans for my concubinage. As I entered, I looked around and saw the formality of the occasion, for no women were present. In attendance were only men, which included the High Priest, one or two of the King's Council, the governor of the city who, because of Tetla's distinguished position within the city government, was to stand as the main witness, several men of my family, and my father. They all stood, as was the custom on formal occasions."

Huitzitzilin paused and gazed at Father Benito, who was scrawling words as rapidly as he could. She cocked her head, expressing interest in what he was doing, then returned to her memories.

"The following words were conveyed by the messenger from his master: 'Hear then, Lady Huitzitzilin, that I, Tetla, chief attendant upon the governor of Tenochtitlan, will take you as a concubine and as part of my household ten days hence. Therefore, let this message be the formal and public confirmation of my intent, as well as the official command that you commence your cleansing in order for you to become part of my family. The preparations will begin at the temple of Tonantzin at daybreak five days from now.'"

Father Benito suddenly stopped writing. "Cleansing? I don't understand."

"Women were considered defiled until cleansed. The Mexica men considered themselves quite pure. Is that so among your own brothers?"

The priest thought that he detected a hint of sarcasm in the woman's words and told himself to be keener in the future. If his was to be a precise chronicle, he needed to identify the times, if any, when Huitzitzilin criticized her own people.

"What did I feel on hearing those words? Well, I cannot remember exactly. I do recall that I felt stiff and cold, and that was probably because I realized that my destiny was somehow encapsulated in those few disdainful words. I remember feeling that I was made of stone, frozen like the snow on the volcanoes, immobile as if my legs had been implanted in the floor on which I stood. I was to become the possession of a man whom I did not know but for whom I was already beginning to feel loathing."

Again, Father Benito halted his pen. "This happens in my land as well. A girl is given to a man and it is expected that happiness will eventually come to her. Surely all women know that one day they will be married."

"Yes. But there is a great difference between knowing and understanding. The gulf between the two can be immense. As I stood there in the center of that room, with so many eyes fixed on me, I understood that I was now a woman, and the pain of that transformation was such that I believed that I would die that very moment."

Huitzitzilin interrupted herself as she listened to the faint pealing of a bell. Father Benito also looked away from his writing and cocked his head toward the metallic clanging. Realizing the time, he jerked his head in her direction. "It is midday. Perhaps we should stop to allow you time to rest and take food."

"No. I'm willing to continue if you are still interested in my story. If not, I can instead make a list of my sins so that you can leave to join your brothers in the monastery."

Father Benito shook his head negatively, letting the woman know that he was more interested in the details she was giving him.

"Allow me then to tell what transpired during those last five days when I was still free. If I were to be asked

37

to point to the most crucial moment of my life, I would indicate those five days. Oh, indeed, I have had many crossroads in my life after that, but as I now look back I see that it was those five days that were the first turning."

"Why were those days so important for you?"

"They were important to all Mexica maidens because they were the days in which a woman was prepared for her husband. For me, they were significant because at their end I would be married to Tetla. He would then discover that I was not a virgin and I was in terror of what he would do. In fact, I considered those days to be my last in this life."

"In Spain, such a husband has the right to kill the woman for deceiving him."

"In the time of the Mexicas this, too, was the man's privilege. However, Tetla was a proud man. To kill me would be to publicly acknowledge his disgrace. I prayed during those days before the ceremony that he would fear the shame of public humiliation and mockery so much that he would keep the truth to himself. For that he would have to let me live. You see, I was torn between the certainly of dying and the hope of living."

Father Benito nodded in understanding, and he was surprised by the compassion he was feeling for Huitzitzilin. He was amazed at himself because he had not imagined that he could sympathize with a woman who had betrayed her husband. In an attempt to shake off the emotion, he changed the direction of her words.

"What did Tetla look like?"

"I thought him very ugly. I was in my fifteenth year and he was much older. He had lewd eyes that looked at me in a repulsive way. Layers of skin rolled over and under those terrible eyes, and even though he wore richly decorated mantles, the blubber of his body was obvious."

"I see. Was a concubine considered less important than a wife, as is the case in my country?"

"No. A man could have numerous wives, and just as many concubines."

Father Benito looked intently at Huitzitzilin, as if trying to untie a stubborn knot. "Then why did a man take a concubine if he could make her his wife? It tells me that somehow the concubine had less importance, less value."

Huitzitzilin wrinkled her brow and pursed her thin lips as she reflected on the monk's words. He thought that she looked like a sparrow.

"I've forgotten the answer to your question. I no longer remember the difference. I do know, however, that the marriage ceremony was the same."

"I'm interested in the ceremony, or whatever ritual took place. Can you remember something about the preparation days?"

The woman hunched deeper into the chair as she intertwined her bony fingers. Her frail body remained with Father Benito, but he understood that her mind had flown to the time of her youth.

"The first day was the day of the girl's dedication to the goddess of the earth and fertility, Tonantzin; the ceremony began at daybreak. The ritual was not long, and it involved the High Priest—how I detested that old snake by the time the five days were over—a few mumbled prayers, little girls that threw flower petals over the head of the young woman, and then the burial of tiny stone replicas of the goddess, thus ensuring fertility for the spouse-to-be."

"You hated the High Priest?" Father Benito was interested in the priestly presence that went on in the lives of the Mexicas, but he was startled at Huitzitzilin's irreverence as she spoke of the man. What if she thought of him, a Catholic priest, in the same manner? He decided to put the thought aside for another time.

"It was at this point of the ceremony that I prayed that my womb not be enriched."

The monk was momentarily taken back by what the woman had said. "You mean the opposite, don't you? You prayed for a fruitful womb."

"No. I meant what I said. I did not want to get impregnated by Tetla. I've already told you that I felt only repulsion for him."

"I see."

"No. You don't see. But we'll leave it as it is."

Huitzitzilin fell into silence, making the priest think that she was displeased with him. He cleared his voice several times, trying to tell her that he was ready to continue.

"On the second day, the future concubine was presented to the king and his council. Her father and the men of her family were present, holding places of honor. The husband to be was required to absent himself from this part of the rite."

40

Father Benito's hand was aching as he tried to record all of Huitzitzilin's words, and he was forced to pause when one of his fingers began to cramp. "Will you allow me a few moments? I'm amazed at your memory."

"I have much to tell you. Some of those things, I'm afraid, you will not want to put into your chronicle."

The priest decided to continue. "What happened on the third day?"

"The third day called for another presentation of the maiden, this time to the future husband and his family, if he had one." Ignoring Father Benito's look of alarm, Huitzitzilin continued. "In Tetla's case, the family included a wrinkled owl, a woman more shriveled and ugly than you now see me. Tetla, although old himself, still had a mother! The family also included his first wife, who was ancient enough to be my grandmother. There were also what seemed to be a countless number of concubines and offspring. I remember the name of only the oldest son, Naxca. He was followed by many other boys and girls of all ages, and the litter finally trailed off to the youngest, a scrawny, crying child.

"The fourth day was the one to select the maiden's wedding garments, as well as the flowers, feathers and gems to be worn on the day of the ceremony. She had to select her personal companions, maidens who would accompany her throughout what was left of the preparations and the ritual itself, and most especially, they were to be by her side as she entered the bridal chamber."

Father Benito whistled softly through his teeth, creating a thin sound. He looked inquisitively at Huitzitzilin.

"Yes. They were supposed to witness the coupling, and they did it gladly. They say that watching such an act can give almost as much pleasure as the copulation itself. I don't know. I've never watched others doing it."

Again, Father Benito lost control over the wave of blood that rushed to his head, making him blush violently. He felt a flash of anger at the woman's way of catching him off guard with such remarks.

Huitzitzilin ignored his agitation and concentrated on describing the dress she had selected. "The gown that I singled out was white cotton, and it draped to my ankles. It was stitched about the sleeves, the collar and along its front with flowers, birds, coiling vines, and leaves. Its colors were blues and reds and greens and yellows and purples."

She glanced at the priest and saw that he was not writing but that he was rubbing his knuckles. She sighed. "I'm tired."

"What about the fifth day? What happened on that day?"

"I thought that you had lost interest in what I was saying."

"Not at all. Please continue."

"Very little happened on that last day except that the maiden spent the time in prayer, fasting, and penance, since the next day would be that of the wedding."

Having said this, Huitzitzilin abruptly stopped speaking and leaned toward the monk. She whispered, "Now I want to continue my confession."

When he deciphered her words, Father Benito jumped, moving so quickly as he reached for the stole that he knocked the papers off his lap. He almost overturned the ink pot, but he was able to steady it before it spilled. After he settled down, he made the sign of the cross.

"Priest, have you absolved me for having done away with the unborn child?"

Benito felt his body tighten because he had thought this part of the confession behind him. He had hoped to lump everything together and not have to say that he pardoned one sin in particular. Nonetheless, even if distasteful, the woman's question forced his hand.

"God forgives you, Señora."

"But do *you* forgive me?"

He stared at her, dumbfounded. Never had a penitent asked such a question of him. Catholics somehow knew, they understood that only God could forgive sin. He resented such a personal question, so he decided to answer with the usual platitude.

"I am an instrument."

"Yes, I know. You said that yesterday. But if your God is willing to forgive me, why not you?"

He paused for several moments that seemed endless to him. He finally blurted out, "I do forgive you. I do!"

Father Benito was shocked to hear his voice utter words his mind had refused to acknowledge, and he felt dejection wrapping itself around him, pressing down on him. He wanted to run away from this woman who had a way of prying out thoughts and feelings of which even he was not aware.

"Good! Now I know that your God has pardoned me. Let us continue tomorrow. I will tell you of my marriage ceremony and of Tetla's rage."

Huitzitzilin stood, swaying slightly. When Father Benito got to his feet, he realized her smallness; she hardly reached the height of his chest. She turned and slowly made her way into the gloom of the cloister.

Chapter
IV

"By the time the sun's first rays fell upon the main square of the city, my ceremonial retinue was ready and waiting. I appeared serene, I'm proud to say, even though my breast felt as if the gods were warring within it. I stood flanked by chosen companions, and I faced the east, waiting for the sun's light to arrive, signaling the giant conch shell to sound."

Father Benito had spent another restless night, but he had arrived at the convent on time, leather pouch in hand, ready to annotate what Huitzitzilin had to say. He was still shaken by the thought of her last words the evening before, but, as it now stood, he could not keep away from her and her narratives.

He observed that the Indian woman appeared to be rested and eager to continue her story. He, on the other hand, felt concerned when he caught on to the pattern of her story. First she spoke of the old ways of the Mexicas, then she surprised him with a sin, one that he was not expecting. How would this day end? he asked himself.

"When the shafts of golden light finally struck the uppermost part of the great pyramid, the conch shell bleated its mournful notes. Then the ceremonial drum boomed out its message that another maiden was to offer herself.

"I was elegant, even resplendent, draped in gold, beautiful feathers and gems. I stood with my eyes riveted on the mountain ridge to the east of the city where I could make out the volcanoes. I imagined the expanses of land that spread beyond them to the jungles, and farther yet to the ocean from where you came."

Father Benito glanced at Huitzitzilin. He took a long, side look, trying to imagine her young and beautiful. What most intrigued him was that what she described had happened before the captains from Spain had discovered this land. He calculated rapidly and concluded that the woman's wedding took place three years before the arrival of Don Hernán Cortés, and thirty-seven years before his own birth. The monk whistled softly, but then was abruptly taken from his figuring by the woman's thin voice.

"The ceremony began. First into the circle of the privileged who assembled at the base of the pyramid was the High Priest and Moctezuma, who blessed me, praying that I would be granted happiness. This, I confess, made me shudder because no one had ever mentioned happiness to me. Not even my mother. Perhaps it was the king's mood at the time because sadness clung to him like a pall. His eyes and lips betrayed it. Remember that there were already signs predicting the end of the fifth sun."

The priest stopped writing. "What signs?"

"There were several. One was an explicable fire that almost destroyed the main temple. Another omen was when dead birds filled the lake. There were tremors, strange tides, and the voice of a wailing woman who cried out for her babes. There were many other signals, but I'm sure your historians have already written about them."

He scratched his chin, thinking. "Yes. Now I remember. Is it true that King Moctezuma was actually waiting for the arrival of our explorers?"

"It is true, and like most everyone else, he thought they were gods. Later on I'll tell you the truth of why he was convinced of that. For the time being, let me continue telling you of the ritual that handed me over to Tetla. The actual contract was a simple thing and consisted of only one gesture. The man took the maiden's hands in his and uttered an agreement to take her as his concubine, to fill her with children, and to feed her.

"The last part of the ceremony is one that will enhance your record. It consisted of a dance in honor of the serpent goddess. It was performed by maidens, twenty or thirty of them, and they were led by my chosen ladies. What a pity that you have taken those practices away from us, because you have not given us anything to replace them."

"If we have asked your people to abandon certain practices, it is because they were rooted in the devil."

"How can anything beautiful be rooted in evil?"

When Father Benito refused to answer, Huitzitzilin returned to what she had been saying.

"The dancing maidens were breathtaking! Together, they formed a myriad of colors, feathers, precious stones and gold. And the sound that they created...oh,...you have never heard anything like it! Each woman had strands of small gourds wrapped around her ankles and wrists; their motion combined to create a bewitching sound. The rhythmic rattle of hundreds of gourds collided against the walls of the temples and pyramids, each time rising up and up until it spiraled heavenward, reaching to the very sun!"

Father Benito stopped writing because he was captivated by the excitement that had overcome Huitzitzilin. She was sitting erect, and she had raised her arms above her head; they were tense, and her outstretched hands seemed to be reaching out to another world. He thought for a moment that he saw her body sway, as if to a beat indistinct to him.

"The dance emulated the undulating of a snake, each girl holding the waist of the one ahead of her. First, the serpent coiled its way down the pyramid from the Sorcerer Bird's temple where the dance had begun. Then it slithered down to the plaza of the square, its many bare feet stomping in cadence with the drums, its shoulders and hips rising and falling softly but firmly. The she-snake then danced in the center of the gawking crowd of lords, nobles, and commoners. The drums heightened their beat, and the serpent followed, more and more rapidly, more and more intensely, hips moving, bellies heaving in and out as if copulating. Soon came the frenzy, the climax, and then an abrupt, jerking stop.

"Then it ended. Although the dance had lasted no more than a short span of time, it left the maidens visibly aroused, their breasts heaving, and the rest of the onlookers seemed ready to pounce one upon the other."

Huitzitzilin slumped into her chair fatigued; she was breathing heavily. After a while she looked at Father Benito and saw that he was staring stonily into space. His face was hard and his lips showed displeasure. He had stopped writing.

"You're displeased?"

"Yes! Now you see why we've condemned your ways?"

"It was a mere ceremonial dance that preceded the marriage act! What can be wrong with such a thing?"

"The marriage act is private, secret, and only the followers of Satan would dare simulate it in public. I cannot write this down, Señora. I would certainly be reprimanded first by my superior and then, God forbid, by the Inquisition."

"How foolish you all are! It was only a dance, I tell you! Nothing more, nothing less. It had nothing to do with your wicked Satan."

Huitzitzilin and Father Benito fell into an angry silence that lasted several minutes; neither wanted to speak. She wrestled with her resentment of his attitude, and he with an intense, uncontrolled physical arousal.

It was Huitzitzilin who finally spoke: "What comes next is what occurred on my marriage night. But before you object because such a description is offensive to Christians, allow me to interject that it is a crucial event in my life, and the sins that I have since then committed hinge on that night. If I do not speak of it, all that will follow will be meaningless to you as my confessor."

"Am I correct in understanding that you are ready to go on with your confession?" The priest spoke through stiffened lips.

"Yes. Put aside your writing instruments because I'm sure that you will consider what I have to say as sinful."

Now Father Benito wanted only to leave the woman's presence. He felt that her words were pushing him closer to the black hole of sin, and he feared for himself. Instead of walking away, however, he reached for his stole.

"In the middle of the revelry that night was a young and beautiful woman who sat still and erect upon her low chair at the head of the banquet room. At her side was an old and obese man; someone repugnant to her. She smiled as she looked out over the heads of the company. Her eyes seemed riveted on a distant point somewhere in space. That beautiful young woman was Huitzitzilin and her eyes were seeing what was to become of her life if she were to live through that night. She was also thinking of Zintle, and of her love for him."

The priest noticed how the woman was referring to herself as if she had been a stranger. Because he was now listening as a confessor, however, he did not interrupt.

"When Tetla had gorged himself with food and drink, he belched loudly, wiped his flaccid mouth, and rolled his eyes in Huitzitzilin's direction. Her heart stopped because she knew that she would soon die or

Song of the Hummingbird

face a worse ordeal! Tetla ordered the accompanying maidens to get to their feet and lead the concubine to the bed chamber. They did so instantly, and as Huitzitzilin followed them, she became aware of the hush that came over the guests. She saw lustful looks being exchanged."

The monk put his hand on the woman's shoulder, trying to convey the sympathy that had inexplicably replaced the anger he had felt a few minutes earlier. He wanted to let her know that he sensed the pain with which she was telling him her story, but he saw that she was transported far back to the past, to a world long since destroyed by the Spanish captains.

"The women companions were supposed to remain to witness the consummation rite, but Tetla ordered them out of the room. Then he tore away Huitzitzilin's gown. She stood before him naked, exposed. He remained standing in front of her, running his eyes up and down her body, pausing at her breasts, her belly, and on her most intimate part. His breathing became thicker and quicker, his vulture's beak pursed.

"Then he pointed to the bed and commanded her to lie on it. She did. Then Tetla stooped low over her and peered into her secret parts. He squinted and strained, and the concubine knew what he was attempting to see. But the light was dim, and his eyes were even dimmer with age and drink, so that he was unable to see if she possessed the membrane that women are born with and to which Mexica men give so much importance.

"Tetla bent even farther down, dipping his face so close to her that she could feel his breath spill over her thighs. She suddenly knew that he was about to plunge

51

his dangling nose into her. Her knees violently snapped shut! They closed hard and viciously upon his head, and she heard by the dull thud that she had caused him much pain.

"'Ahg!' he groaned as he reeled backward. He stood dazed, attempting to regain his balance by pressing back against the wall. Huitzitzilin was filled with terror, and like those insects that skitter on the sands of a river, she rolled herself into a ball. But Tetla composed himself and returned to her, forcing her to open her body to him. Then he violated the concubine.

"She thought that it was over, that she was about to die, but it wasn't, because Tetla chose not to kill her. Instead he battered her. His blows fell on her like rocks. His fists hammered at her head, face, body, anywhere they found a spot. He threw her off the bed, stomped his feet on her shoulders and buttocks. His fingers coiled themselves around her hair, and he dragged her around the room. Then he picked her up like a sack of maize and threw her against the wall, bouncing her back and forth, smashing her face against any surface that he could find. Tetla did that and many other things over and again, and he did it silently, without uttering a word or sound.

"The concubine remained silent also, but the pain became more unbearable with each moment. Her breath became slower, and the light began to grow dimmer. All she could hear was Tetla's breathing and her own throat gasping for air. Then, as if in the hollow of concentric circles, she began to sink and slip down...down...down... to Mictlan, to the land of the dead, and deeper still...

down and down...even beyond the kingdom where your own prince Lucifer lurks...down...until she landed in the pit of all pits, and there was total darkness."

The woman's voice trailed to a hoarse whisper until it stilled. Father Benito was silent. He was so filled with her pain that he could not speak. He saw that she was moved by what she had just told him and that she was shivering. He tried to help by adjusting the thin shawl closer to her shoulders, but when it did not help, he put his head close to hers.

"This is not your sin. It was his alone. I know that in my country a man would have done the same to a woman, but still, it is his sin, and not the woman's. May I ask you to forgive him now so that the anguish might disappear?"

"It happened to her, not to me. It is she who must forgive Tetla for what he did."

Father Benito stared at Huitzitzilin, trying to understand her meaning. Then, wrinkling his brow with incomprehension, he nodded, got to his feet, and walked away from her.

Father Benito sat quietly in the leather and wood
armchair near the fireplace; the flickering flames in the
hearth held his gaze. He was in the monastery library
facing his confessor Father Anselmo Cano, who sat holding his thin hand to the side of his face. In the glow of
the fire, his tapered fingers threw shadows on his bony
forehead and on the pointed cowl covering his head.
Looking away from the fire, Benito had the impression
that the countless books surrounding them moved in
rhythm with the reflections cast by the fire.

Both monks were quiet for a long time, and their
silence was broken only by the sputtering of burning
logs. It was Benito who finally spoke up.

"As I've said, Father, I can repeat what I heard this
afternoon because it was not truly a confession. The
Indian woman told me first of her wedding ceremony,
and then of the beating she suffered at the hands of the
groom."

"I see, and I agree that you're not breaking the seal
of the confessional. But I see that you're in turmoil,
Brother, and that you would not be here at this moment

except that you're looking for my assistance. Tell me how I can help. After all, it was I who advised you to continue your conversations with the woman."

Benito sighed deeply, conveying his confusion. "When she described the ordeal she suffered at the hands of her husband, the woman spoke of herself as if being someone else."

"How so?"

"She spoke always of *the* Concubine. Not once did she say me or I. Do you understand me, Reverend Father?"

"I understand your words, but I cannot explain why anyone would speak in that fashion." Father Anselmo stopped abruptly. "Unless she speaks in that manner always. Is that the case?"

"No. Only when she spoke of that incident did she revert to such a distant way of describing what happened to her."

The monks returned to their silence. This time Father Anselmo had his elbows on the armrests and held both hands together at the fingertips, as if in prayer. Father Benito sat with his hands in his lap. It had grown dark out, and only the muffled sounds coming from the brothers in the kitchen could be made out, interspersed by the distant barking of a dog.

"She has told you much about her people?"

"Yes, Father."

"New information, by your reckoning?"

"Very new."

"Can you give me an example?"

"Gladly! She has described certain events and occurrences that have centered on King Moctezuma. She has been able to tell of the clothing he wore and what he said at such times. To my memory, no one has chronicled similar information."

"I see." Father Anselmo was evidently pondering what next to say. "What else has she said that you consider valuable?"

"Let me see." The young monk reflected for a moment. "I have much already written, but other examples that now come to mind are her willingness to describe the city as it was before its conquest."

"Captain Cortés has done as much."

"Of course, Reverend Father, but the woman is able to describe what the captain did not. She tells of the way ordinary rooms and palaces were kept. She has also described, just today, a ritualistic dance that I'm positive our people never witnessed. Also, she has made several references to the true reasons of why her people expected us. This, I know, we have not yet recorded."

The older monk returned to his thoughts for a long while, and then spoke. "It seems that your time is being well spent. But why are you agitated and worried? What is it about the Indian woman that disturbs you?"

Father Benito flinched as if Anselmo had pricked him with a pin; the question had hit its mark. "It's the inexplicable way in which she tells her sins. A way that is not marked by repentance, but rather as if her actions had been mere happenstance. She expresses herself in a way that makes me begin to wonder if what she has done is sinful or not."

Father Anselmo showed his alarm at what Benito had said by suddenly dropping his arms on his lap. "Father, please! Never, never repeat that to anyone, even if you do believe it! Walls have ears, you know, and the Inquisition is ever alert to ferret out heretics."

The priest sat back, giving himself time to regain balance, then he continued, his eyes locked on those of Father Benito. "You did not utter those words! I did not hear them! Do you grasp my meaning, Brother?"

"Yes, Father." Benito's voice was hushed fearfully.

"Is the woman a baptized Christian?"

"I believe so."

"You believe so? Are you not certain?"

"Well...I mean...she's in the protection of the convent."

"That means nothing!"

"She voluntarily asked to confess."

"She could be laying a snare for you!"

"Father, she bears a Christian name."

"What is that name?"

Shaken, Father Benito realized with alarm that he didn't know her name, except that of Hummingbird. He concluded that to reveal that the woman's name was that of a bird would not be wise at this moment already filled with uncertainty.

"I'm not sure, but I'll find out tomorrow."

Father Anselmo sighed, expressing exasperation. "I'll grant you permission to continue meeting with the woman under certain conditions. You must, first of all, prepare yourself to distinguish between what was purely tribal tradition and what was religious ritual. Never,

never allow the woman to allude to the demons that were the mainspring of their so-called religion. You must remember that her people were steeped in witchcraft and possessed the means to conjure demonic powers."

The younger priest swallowed hard, remembering that he had already trespassed this injunction. Benito nervously returned his attention to Father Anselmo who had paused, sucking in a large gulp of air. He cocked his head, narrowed his eyes, and then went on. "Perhaps the enigmatic way in which she described her wedding night is the beginning of a hex; the first signs of sorcery. It's possible."

"I don't believe that, Father, but I will abide by your counsel."

"Very well." Anselmo paused as he scratched his chin; he appeared to be weighing one thought against the other. He finally spoke. "I'll trust in you, Benito. However, I have a second condition. You mustn't feel pity or sympathy for her previous ways, or those of her people. We have brought them redemption, don't forget that. We can't allow them to relapse."

"No, Father, I won't forget, and I accept this condition also." He closed his eyes, recalling the feelings of compassion he had already experienced for Huitzitzilin.

Father Anselmo nodded distractedly; he was thinking of something else. "I shall never be able to fathom why people—we and they—each so diverse in all ways, have crossed paths. Who will ever know why each of our nations, separated by vast oceans, unknowing of the existence of the other until now, have come together.

What could be the reason, except that Our Lord Savior willed it."

"Amen!" Benito made the sign of the cross. "Does this, then, not prove that they are human beings like us?"

The older monk stared at Benito, his eyes were bright with a mix of surprise and understanding. Both men were thinking of the now historic debates that had taken place in the universities of Spain. Were the inhabitants of this land human beings or mere creatures to be held as chattels? went the argument.

Father Anselmo stood quietly and walked to the door. The conference had ended. He seemed to glide over the polished floor tiles, and the hem of his habit made a light whipping sound as it wrapped around his ankles. When he reached the door, he put his hand on the knob as he turned to face the young monk. "Of course they're human. The difference between them and us, however, is that we are the instrument of their salvation."

Chapter VI

Next morning, before sitting next to her, Father Benito pressed Huitzitzilin with a series of questions he had prepared.

"Señora, are you a baptized Christian?"

She looked at him; a combination of amusement and curiosity were reflected on her face. When she didn't answer, he sat in the chair, paused, and changed the question.

"What is your baptismal name?"

Huitzitzilin looked away from the monk before answering. "Don't you know that we were all baptized by your missionaries? It was done in groups of dozens, even hundreds."

Benito cursed himself for sounding stupid; of course he knew the procedure. The natives had all been christened at the beginning, except for those who had fled.

"Yes...yes, of course. I knew that." He stuttered his words. "Tell me, then, what is your real name?" The woman's face whipped around to face him and, realizing what she was about to say, he countered. "No! Not the bird name! I want to know your Christian name."

"María de Belén."

Huitzitzilin's voice was so low that Benito, even though hunched in her direction, could not hear her response.

"What did you say?"

The woman jerked her arms towards the monk, hands rolled into fists, and her toothless mouth opened wide, forming a black rectangle. Benito caught a glimpse of its tiny, pink tongue before he was jolted by the unexpectedly strong voice that rang out.

"Ma-rí-a-a-a!"

She shouted the word. Its vibration crackled with irritation as it echoed through the silent cloister halls.

Father Benito jerked back, nearly loosing his balance, but after a few seconds, when he regained his composure, he was at least satisfied that she was a baptized Christian and that she had a suitable name. Pursing his lips and rubbing the palms of his hands together, he showed relief.

"Shall we begin?"

He gingerly reached for paper and quill, settled himself in the chair and prepared to write. But he soon looked up and noticed that she was slumped in her chair, looking grumpy.

"Have I upset you?"

"Yes!"

"It's my obligation to know these things about you."

"What things?"

"That you have a Christian name."

"You mean you have to make sure that I have been robbed of everything, even my name."

Father Benito was dismayed. He had not imagined that the old woman had such mettle, nor that she could be so outspoken. Her irascibility had cropped up before, but not so shrilly as now. He decided that it would be better not to pursue the matter.

"Please! Let's continue with your story. Tell me what happened to you after that dreadful night. How and who nursed you back to health?"

"You have many questions today, don't you?"

Benito looked at her. His expression was sheepish, but he realized with surprise that her testiness did not annoy him, that he was growing fond of her and her manner. But Father Anselmo's words came back to him, and he made a firm decision to try to put aside sentiment with the Indian woman.

She began to speak. "I cannot say how many days and nights I was trapped in the underbelly of the world, but it was a time of intense battle for me. Unconscious, I grappled with demons, I combated with grinning skulls, I wrestled with monsters that bit and stung my flesh. During my stupor, there was only terror to keep me company, only fear that compelled me to continue on the path that would take me back to life. But I was trapped in a maze of pain and grief, and I did not want to recover consciousness because I felt that worse things awaited me up there where the sun was shining."

Benito noted that Huitzitzilin no longer spoke of herself as a stranger. He decided not to pursue the matter, relieved because this disproved Anselmo's claim of a possible hex.

"It was a grim road, and even though senseless, I saw that my feet left bloody prints as I walked, stamps that transformed themselves into demons that trailed after me in constant attack. My heart ached, my spirit wept, and my body desired death. When I did re-enter this world, it was only to find myself crushed and scarred, my face swollen beyond recognition, and I desired death more than ever.

"Then slowly my spirit took hold of itself, raising itself out of that pain and misery and humiliation. A tiny fire, a speck in the beginning, was born in the center of my brain, drawing life, growing until it became a powerful flame that carried my spirit up and out of my torment. I was alive, and never again would this happen to me. When I opened my eyes, I realized that I would be free because pain had liberated me."

Father Benito could not refrain from interrupting her. "I've never heard such talk before."

"You find it strange?"

"Yes, because we all suffer pain, and yet none of us is free."

The woman began to cry, and Father Benito became alarmed, not knowing what had brought it on. He put his papers aside and awkwardly placed his hand on hers.

"I cannot help it. I weep for myself, for my children, and for the daughter who doesn't know who her mother is."

"You had children?" His voice was charged with disbelief.

She nodded but said nothing more. A few moments passed until the monk again took paper in hand, wondering how many other mysteries were buried in the woman's memory. He decided not to pry; instead he would wait until she was ready to speak about what had made her cry so unexpectedly.

"I returned to the land of the living. My ladies had nursed me, forcing the juices of meats and fruits through my lips. They washed and made sure that my body was placed in different positions in the bed. During those days in which my spirit floundered in the bowels of the earth, my maidens had cared for my body.

"When I finally revived, I was told what had happened after I lost consciousness. Tetla had walked away from me, confident that I would die. When he discovered that I had survived, he instructed the servants to keep me in his palace until he returned."

Huitzitzilin noticed that the monk was not writing, so she stopped speaking. She stared at him but saw that he was rubbing his hands, palm against palm, in apparent distraction.

"You're not writing. Are you not interested?"

Father Benito squirmed in the chair; he seemed not to know what to say.

"I...I'm sorry, Señora. The truth is that I am interested. However, I'm here for one of two things. That is, either I should be recording what you have to say of the previous ways of your people, or hear your confession. I believe what you're now telling is neither."

"I see. Does it not matter to you that I had a child?"

"Matter? Of course it matters! Was it from Tetla?"

"No. At first he thought it was, but the truth was that the father of the boy was Zintle."

"Oh!" The priest's voice dipped.

"I suppose this is a matter for confession?"

"The child was conceived out of wedlock. That is a sin."

"How many times must a person confess the same sin?"

Father Benito held his breath, suspecting another of the woman's surprise moves that breached the gap between Mexica ritual and Christian theology. He answered as he had been taught to respond.

"As many times as that sin is committed."

"Even if its the same sin done with the same person?"

"Yes."

"Then I confess to you..."

Father Benito nervously threw his documentation aside, scattering the pages on the floor. He fumbled, reaching for the stole necessary to hear a confession.

"...that I made love to Zintle many times, in many places until I became pregnant again. We did this while Tetla was away."

She had blurted out her sin faster than Benito could prepare himself. Although too late, he went through the motions, making the sign of the cross and settling in the posture he always took to hear a confession.

"I'm finished. There is no more. Should I repeat my sin again so it will count now that you're ready?"

He flushed heavily, convinced that she was mocking him. He yanked away the stole, gathered his things, and without saying anything began to leave the cloister. He felt humiliated by the woman and by his own clumsiness; this angered him.

"Will you return tomorrow? I'll tell you of one of the first encounters of our people with yours."

Father Benito thought that he detected an apology in the woman's tone. He stopped and turned to look at her, and saw that in the closing darkness Huitzitzilin looked as if carved in stone, she seemed so ancient. The impression moved him, dispelling the irritation her surprise confession had caused in him.

"Yes. I'll return."

Chapter
VII

"As I promised yesterday, young priest, I'll now tell you of the first signs we had of the coming of your people. First, however, I want to assure you that I won't be telling you of my sinful ways anymore. That is, not until the end. At that time, I'll warn you with time so that you can prepare yourself."

Grateful to see that the woman had noticed his turmoil the day before and relieved to know that he would not have to worry about theological matters, Father Benito's interest was immediately engaged by the prospect of being the first to hear new information. He was certain that few chronicles held the experiences of one such as this Indian woman.

"I know that this part will be of interest to you because it involves one of your own. As it turns out, Tetla was called to the eastern coast because strange events were occurring, and tributary tribes had reported the presence of a strange, pale creature who had been enslaved by one of the Maya villages. Moctezuma was by that time worried by the many portents that had made themselves manifest in his kingdom. When he received notice of the appearance of the creature, he was shaken.

"The reports also stated that when the man had been found, he was accompanied by another who was created in the same mold and whose skin was of the same pallid color; both of them stank intolerably."

"They stank? Were they sick?"

"No. All of you smell in a peculiar way, so I suppose it's something with which you're born."

Father Benito recoiled, hugging his arms to his sides, conscious of the odor that his armpits gave off. He often went without bathing for long periods of time.

She smiled wryly. "No. You can't help it. All of you smell." Huitzitzilin said this casually before going on. "The circumstances of their arrival were equally disconcerting. Moctezuma had been advised that those creatures had emerged from a huge structure, a large house, with white wings, that glided on the water. However, in this instance, something had gone wrong, because the thing had collided and floundered against the rocks of the coast. Then, as if vomiting its insides out, the floating monster spat out several white creatures. They died almost immediately; only two survived."

Father Benito put down the quill and squinted his eyes as he remembered. This was not new. The two men she was talking about were by now famous in Spain. His memory groped, trying to come up with their names. However, he could recall only one of them, Jerónimo de Aguilar.

The monk remembered that this man had been shipwrecked onto this land almost ten years before Captain Cortés, and that by the time Aguilar was rescued by the Spaniards, he already knew how to speak the language of the people who had captured him. What no one knew, however, was what had become of the man.

"Does anyone know what happened to Aguilar?"

"Yes. He died a very old man, a monk I believe, in the Convent of San Juan Baptista here in Coyoacán. It is a refuge for aged priests. It is not far from here. He died recently, no more than five years ago."

Father Benito made a note to visit the place and see if he could come up with more facts. He shook his head, not understanding how this material had not reached Spain. And yet this woman knew of it.

"That man was important to your captains because he was the one who became the first interpreter for Don Hernán Cortés on his progress in this direction.

"There was a woman, also. She was young at the time and she soon replaced Aguilar as interpreter. She was known as Malinche. She became Cortés' mistress and bore him a son."

This, too, had already been recorded and included in the instructional sessions of all missionaries coming to this land. But Father Benito wanted to know more about that woman; what had not been part of the chronicles.

"What happened to her?"

"Few people know that after Cortés passed her on to another of his captains, she fled rather than accept that humiliation. Most Mexicas saw her as a traitor, and few people had compassion for her. I heard recently that she died, but that she had lived a serene life because she did not see herself as a traitor. And I agree! She wasn't even a Mexica!"

Father Benito was writing as rapidly as possible. When he scrawled the last word, he turned to Huitzitzilin, wanting more information about the concubine.

"I feel glad for her."

"Why?"

"Because she did what her heart and mind told her to do. And because I did many things that she did. Our lives are very similar."

Benito wrinkled his forehead. He was on the verge of asking Huitzitzilin to explain, but she rambled on.

"At that time I was invited by Moctezuma's wife, Yani, to be one of her women companions. I mention this because not only was it a position of privilege, but it put me in a place where I was able to observe many important events as well. I know that this is important to your record. I, among others, witnessed the collapse of our kingdom from a close view."

"I want you to tell me everything you can remember about those days."

"But you already know everything."

"Not from your way of seeing those events."

"Then you must know that it was during those days that I gave birth to a son."

"Zintle's?"

"Yes. I named the boy... No, I won't say it in my language since I see it troubles your tongue. I named him Wing of a Bird."

The woman leaned deep into the chair. She was lost in thought, but Father Benito waited until she resumed speaking. She returned to the present with a start.

"Many years have passed since the child's birth, so much has happened since then, yet I see it all with the clarity of yesterday's events. The omens continued to occur near the eastern coast. In truth, several years passed as these things took place. It was as the god Quetzalcóatl, the preacher god, had foretold in ages..."

"No! Don't mention the idols!"

Father Benito's voice trembled, betraying the fear the god's name conjured in his mind.

"No? But if you don't allow me to speak of them, how can I explain the most important part of those events?"

The monk was dumbfounded. Yet he had promised Father Anselmo that he would not allow allusion to those demons. He bit his lip in consternation because he couldn't help thinking that it would be equally difficult to speak of his own people without the mention of Jesus Christ.

His eyes widened in shock, and he made the sign of the cross, realizing that he had actually compared the Savior to an idol. Benito was struck with horror at how close he had come to blasphemy.

"What is the matter? Are you ill?"

"No! I'm not. I'm just fatigued. You must give me a few moments to gather my thoughts."

Saying this, Benito stood and walked to the fountain. There he splashed water on his fevered face while he wrestled with what to do next. When he looked over his shoulder, he saw that the Indian woman was gazing at him, and again he thought that she looked like an idol.

He stood by the fountain not knowing what to do, when he saw that she was signaling him to return to her side. He was afraid. Was Satan working through her? he wondered. He waited for the answer, as if it would come to him from heaven. But then he reminded himself that he was looking at a frail old woman, and that she could not possibly harm him or his spirit. Feeling ashamed of his thoughts, he decided to go back to her.

"Think as you would of two opposing factions: one interested in gaining personal power and wealth through war yet calling it religion, and the other as being faithful to the principle of peace at all costs. Does that not happen in your land?"

"Sometimes."

"Then I'll refer only to the war and peace parties."

Relieved, Father Benito returned to his place as he gathered his material. The woman had stated the matter clearly and logically, and now he wondered why he had reacted so violently in the first place. Also, he noted, this was indeed the first time he had heard of the issues of her people put in terms of war and peace, not demons and gods.

"As I was about to say, Moctezuma was a member of the war group; he was, in fact, the main priest. He was a complicated man because, as it turned out, in his heart he had always feared that the peace message held by the early Mexicas and abandoned by their later descendants would one day return to haunt him. Now we all know that he secretly considered himself a traitor, and that every time a sign appeared to the east, he became more convinced that the era of the war party was at an end.

"The king kept these thoughts buried deep within himself. The result was that his uncertain behavior was misunderstood; it cast doubt on his courage. He tried to explain his gifts of gold and gems as mere tribute to passing visitors, but instead his actions were interpreted as cowardly. The war party increased its demand that he send warriors to destroy the intruders. He would not listen to them, much less conform.

"In my position so close to Moctezuma's wife, I was able to see a side of him few people could understand. He could be honest or cagey, decisive or hesitant, brave or faint-hearted. But whatever others said, he was king.

"I remember that during those fearful days, he was constantly receiving reports from the widespread net of informers in his service. Word reached this city on a daily basis telling of your people, what they looked like, how they spoke and about the four-legged beasts they rode."

Father Benito ran his tongue over his upper lip in excitement because he knew that he was gathering information not yet recorded in Spain. He was seeing the events of the conquest through the eyes of the Indian woman, and even though he wanted to hear more of her life's story, he decided not to interrupt while she narrated details regarding that historic encounter.

"Remember Tetla? Well, let me tell you how much my own life was intertwined with the events that brought about our end."

The priest shook his head, wondering when this woman would stop amazing him. It was as if she had read his thoughts.

"Moctezuma depended on Tetla for information because he was gifted in languages and knowledge of the tribes of the eastern coast. It was he who brought the report giving the first picture of what the foreigners looked like. Now that we know you so well, you don't seem that strange. But at that time..."

Benito looked at Huitzitzilin, no longer resisting the understanding that was growing in him. He realized that she, too, had seemed strange to him just a few days before, but now she was becoming more like any other woman.

"Those of us who belonged to the king's court heard Tetla confirm the reports regarding your ships, and how they housed dozens of men who made their way to the shore on smaller boats. He was one of the few who actually got close enough to them to see that their skin was so pale that it appeared transparent. At this point in his description, I remember that most of us let out gasps of disbelief, but the rest of the picture was even more frightening.

"He told of how not only their heads, but their chins as well, were covered all over with hair. On some of them that growth was light and curled, and on others it was darker and sleek. Their dress, he said, was fashioned of some form of silver, or metal, which shone in the sun, and they carried armaments, some that resembled our own, and others which Tetla could not describe.

"Through it all, Moctezuma became more convinced that those foreigners were the representatives of the feared preacher chief, the leader of the peace party. Did you know that among the many omens received through previous generations of priests, descriptions of what the peace mongers would look like had been passed down? And even more important, those portrayals matched that of the first captains, as did the very date foretold by our visionaries. Did you know this, young priest?"

Benito shook his head.

The woman rubbed her hands in satisfaction, understanding that she was the one who knew the truth, and that the monk saw it as valuable. It was a twist, and she was appreciating it.

"After that, Tetla returned to the eastern coast and I never saw him until the day of his death. I'll tell you about that later on. As of the moment, however, I think you'll be interested to hear of how those events affected Moctezuma.

"I saw him often and he appeared distracted, dazed even. His wife told me on several occasions that she had found him muttering to himself as he stalked hallways and chambers, wringing his hands and lifting his eyes to heaven, imploring help from the gods."

Huitzitzilin stopped speaking for a moment, then said, almost in a whisper, "He was just flesh and blood, but he had been made to believe that he was divine." She looked over at Father Benito, but saw that he was writing so intently that he didn't notice her emotion.

"Moctezuma deteriorated with each moment. He went into mourning and commanded us all—the entire city—to do likewise and to be ready for the calamitous days that would certainly come. It was common knowledge by then that he spent long hours in prayer, fasting, and penance, and that he personally sacrificed human offerings, hoping..."

Benito's face blanched. He had been feeling sympathy for the king until that moment. He stopped writing, allowing the quill to dangle from his fingers as he rolled his eyes from one side of the cloister to the other.

"Are you sure?" The monk's voice was husky with disbelief. "Did the king really commit such atrocities with his own hand?"

"Human offerings were part of our beliefs. You have yours."

Her words were soft, sincere, unchallenging, and they helped restore Benito's serenity. "Yes, Señora, and I would hope that by now my beliefs have replaced yours."

He heard her sigh, but she said nothing.

"A pall hung over Tenochtitlan those days, and no one could dispel or ignore the abiding, sickening feeling that soon, very soon, something disastrous would unleash itself upon us.

"Have you noticed, young priest, how people act when expecting something?" Huitzitzilin's voice took on a lighter tone. "If that something is unknown, people invent things to do, games to play, excursions to take. Tempers often become prickly. Men and women overindulge in food and drink, and suffer headaches or stomach discomfort. They develop loose bowels, or uncooperative ones. Gossip becomes intolerable.

Song of the Hummingbird

"Such was our life in Tenochtitlan those last days of our world. The soft rain passed to heat, and that to the cold with its shortened days, and thus to the end of the year which to you was 1518.

"Some people were disbelieving of what was happening. They attempted to convince others that a misreading of the signs had occurred on the part of the augurs. They insisted that the signs were symbolic, or merely ritualistic, and that such events had already occurred during other eras. But to be honest, by the time Captain Cortés made his presence, everyone believed that the white men were either gods or their emissaries, and that conviction never changed or disappeared until it was too late to halt them.

"Much bickering and quarreling took place regarding what was to be done with the intruders. One side clamored for their destruction; the other for their appeasement. In the end it mattered little. War or worship, it concluded as foretold. Our world terminated the moment the first white man set foot on our land, and I believe now that Moctezuma was the only one who truly saw that irreversible truth."

Chapter
VIII

It took a long time for the gatekeeper to open the convent door for Father Benito. He didn't mind because the autumn morning was mild; the usual chill was missing, and so he waited patiently, thinking of what another day with the Indian woman would be like. He looked in different directions as he distractedly whistled under his breath.

He tried to imagine how much had changed in this city since her youth. The woman had told of an ancestral home, where she had been born and which was now the site of this convent. She had spoken of the Hill of the Stars, Iztapalapa, a sacred place to her people but which was these days an open market bustling with Spanish-speaking merchants and buyers. She had described the main temple, and Benito thought of the cathedral taking its place; its twin spires now dominating houses built in the Spanish manner.

He pulled on the bell cord again, impatiently this time, making the clanging metal sound out shrilly. But no one responded. He rearranged the strap of his leather case because it was beginning to cut into his shoulder, then he took a few paces away from the entrance. Two native boys startled him as they came around the corner, prodding a donkey loaded with hay. He noticed their faces as they trotted by him: round, brown faces. Then, as if pulled by a string, the boys turned in his direction; he saw the flinty, oval-shaped eyes gazing at him.

"*¡Buenos días, Padre!*"

"*¡Buenos días, Niños!*"

They disappeared in seconds, leaving the monk amazed at himself for having, for the first time since his arrival in Tenochtitlan, seen how different the boys were one from the other. Even though they seemed of an age, and had the same color, they were distinct. This had not yet occurred to him because, up until then, all those faces had blurred into one.

Now he wanted to run after them to ask if their fathers remembered the same things as did the Indian woman. But then Father Benito realized that it would have been their grandfathers instead who would have such memories, maybe even more likely their great-grandfathers.

Suddenly, the monk wished that he had been born sixty years sooner so that he could have seen the city as it was during the days of the Indian woman's people, of the great-grandfathers of those boys. He stared in concentration at his feet: his callused toes peeked out from under the leather thongs of worn-out sandals.

A thought was taking shape in his mind as he fixed his eyes on one of the straps. Slowly, an idea crept forward into his consciousness, and he finally understood that something deep within him was beginning to share

Huitzitzilin's melancholy for what was irrevocably gone. This impulse took Father Benito by surprise, and he shook his head trying to take a fresh approach to his mission. He was in this land to convert, not to be converted, he told himself.

Because he was lost in his thought, Father Benito was startled by the heavy hand that suddenly tugged at his arm. He twirled around to see who was pulling him with such energy, and he was greeted by the tiny eyes of the nun who usually opened the convent doors.

Chapter IX

"They came!

"Moctezuma had prayed that they would not come, but his petitions were futile, because they did come. The moment finally came when your captains stood knocking at the gates of Tenochtitlan, and we were powerless to stop them from entering.

"When that day dawned, the priests approached our king to inform him of the white intruders who awaited him in Iztapalapa. Later on we heard that Moctezuma was sweeping the stairs of the temple, and that without looking up, he said, 'The gods have failed me.' That was all he said, no more."

Father Benito felt a tingle on the nape of his neck, as if he had been present at a disastrous event. He was feeling what he thought Huitzitzilin must have felt at the time. Like her and her people, he was experiencing the fear of the unknown, as if he had been a native himself. He forced himself to return to his writing because, he reminded himself, these were the captains from Spain, his people, and he should not be feeling such antagonism towards them.

"We all knew that the king was grief-stricken, but there were some among our people who murmured that it was the other way around. That it had been he who had failed the gods, and that now the gods were rightfully vengeful.

"Priest, have you observed that events of great import often take a very short span of time to happen? The fall of Tenochtitlan was quick. From beginning to end, our finality spanned just a few weeks and months, and what had taken my people ages to build, was brought low with a few battles.

"Our temples, palaces, market places, meeting halls, schools and libraries, our thoroughfares and gardens and squares, all destroyed in a brief time. Our trade routes, goods, and products were laid in the mud and trampled by the feet of beasts in the time taken to hear a clap of hands. Our crafts and art, all of which took countless families and immeasurable time to perfect, were scorned, defiled, and made to disappear by your captains in a few passings of the moon.

"I ask myself now, how is it possible to destroy so swiftly what took years to build? I have no answer, but that it happened as the gods had determined. Tenochtitlan crashed down amid fire and blood and anguish, and it took only a scattering of days."

"Forgive my interruption, but this shows that it was the will of Almighty God that the kingdom of the Mexicas should have perished."

Putting aside his sentiments, Father Benito, eyebrows arched, mouthed what he thought the most appropriate thing. Huitzitzilin looked at him in silence for a long while, then spoke.

"Yes, I agree. I said so a few moments ago. It was as the gods willed."

Benito frowned, annoyed that the woman should insist on putting her gods on the same level with the one true God, but he took up his quill once again nonetheless. He was ready to continue recording her words.

"I remember clearly the day of the arrival of the white men. It took place during the season of dampness in our valley. It was the time when days were short, when the lake turned black in color, and the winds swept off the skirts of the volcanoes.

"Moctezuma's court became agitated. Word of the arrival of the white men went from mouth to mouth, from chamber to chamber. Men and women ran around aimlessly as if that would resolve the impending doom. Routines were broken and duties forgotten. Incredulous faces looked around, seeking answers, hoping to hear that what was happening was nothing more than a hoax.

"The noise caused by the confused masses of people in the main square rose to a pitch with each minute. There, men attempted to appear calm, but trembling lips betrayed their fears. Women tried to console themselves by embracing babies, or each other, but it was no use. We were all in the grip of terror."

Father Benito, compelled by surprise, interrupted again. "Yet, the Mexicas were ferocious in battle. It has never occurred to us that the people were stricken by fear all along."

"You misunderstand me, priest! When I say that we were alarmed, I mean that most of the people assumed that the visitors were gods, not ordinary men. Had they been the hordes of Zapotecas, or Tlaxcaltecas, or any other of the countless peoples that had waged war against us, our spirits would not have been so shaken. We felt terror only because we thought we were facing the unknown. When it became clear that your captains were just men, things changed."

The monk sucked on his lower lip while he wrinkled his forehead. "I see what you mean. Please go on."

"The order came from the king telling us to stop the madness, to take hold of ourselves. He commanded each one of us to dress in our best garments and to accompany him to the entrance of the city."

"Did everyone do as the king commanded?"

"Yes. Most of us were part of his court and we did as he ordered. We dressed in our finest clothing so that we could walk behind his litter and impress the enemy by our appearance."

"Am I correct in saying that you were among those who did not believe the soldiers were gods?"

"Yes. I was among those who knew them to be flesh, just as we were."

Benito cocked one eyebrow skeptically. "What made you so different, Señora?" There was a note of sarcasm in his voice.

"Because I never really believed in gods."

"But you believe in the one true God now, don't you?"

The monk's words had lost all trace of cynicism and were now colored with doubt.

"If you say so."

When Benito remained silent, Huitzitzilin went on. "One extraordinary thing happened as a result of the fear caused by your people, and that was that old feuds and envies disappeared. Those among us who had been enemies for generations forgot their grudges and joined one another against the invasion.

"For example, the hostility between the pampered dwarfs and the rancorous eunuchs melted away. They actually came together, speaking to one another. Priests and conjurers alike were struck dumb knowing that gods were at the city entrance. Their usual jabbering and high-pitched squealing melted into a muted stiffness, and we all knew that in their hearts they were the most frightened of all. Where was their power now? Where was their magic? Where was their stiff-necked pride and intolerable arrogance?"

Father Benito stopped to rub his fingers; they were beginning to cramp again. "I see that you didn't believe in the sorcerers you called priests, either. I'm glad because I'm sure it was the true God that planted those doubts in your heart."

"No, that was not the case. I didn't believe in them because I had eyes that perceived their wickedness and ears that heard their conniving and trickery. I knew that they were frauds—it's that simple. But let me go on because I have to tell you that fear struck beyond the priesthood, contaminating even the palace guards, who didn't know whether to run or stand, protect the king or each other. Soldiers trained in war and combat became like motherless boys when they heard that the white gods were here.

"Palace servants forgot their place. Moctezuma's tailors scattered and ran about muttering, asking if the king were ever again to dress as he used to. What would they do with the mantles, the loincloths, the headdresses, the sandals, the gems, the feathers, the broaches, the leg wrappings as yet not worn by the king? What would he wear that day? What should he wear when facing gods?

"Even Moctezuma's cooks ran through chambers and halls wringing their hands. They, too, were in turmoil. Would the king ever again eat as he was accustomed? What would happen to the quail, rabbits, and the other meats preserved and prepared for him? What about his usual guests? What would they be told? What about Moctezuma's next cup of chocolate?

"Now that I think of those days, I wonder why we wasted our time on such trivialities. But it hit everyone. Gardeners, builders and slaves roamed through squares and kitchens asking if they would ever again be employed, now that our world had come to an end. What type of work, they inquired, would the new masters demand of them? Would they eat off gold plates? asked the kitchen servants. Would they enjoy the beauty of the flowers that the king loved? The builders wanted to know what would happen to the plans for the new reservoir. As for the slaves, they asked whether or not the new gods would expect them to work. This was the havoc that reigned in Moctezuma's palace and city while your captains waited at its door and dreamed of our gold."

After saying this, the woman fell into silence while sounds of bubbling water floated in the moist cloister air. Father Benito put down his quill, allowing Huitzitzilin to rest, but he was agitated by the pictures her words had conjured in his imagination. He was envisioning Captain Cortés, the medium-sized man who had become a giant in Spain. He was remembering the other captains who had become wealthy on the bounty carved out of this land. Some had remained rich until the end of their days; others had lost everything, dying impoverished and forgotten.

He was grateful for the lull in the narrative because it gave him time to sort out what Huitzitzilin had said about the terror and confusion that had taken hold of the Mexicas at the time of that crisis. He had never thought of what it must have been like for them. From childhood, Benito had seen her people as the enemy, devil worshipers incapable of fear and uncertainty.

"Do you want me to continue?"

Father Benito was startled by Huitzitzilin's words. He nodded, but he had lost the quill and, even though he fumbled in the folds of his habit, he couldn't find it. She waited patiently until he located it.

"Our procession began at the main temple and wound its way toward Iztapalapa, whose king at the time was Moctezuma's brother, Cuitlahuac."

"Just a moment. How many kings were there?"

"Several. Cuauhtémoc was king of Tlaltelolco, the place where a Christian church has now been dedicated to Santiago of Compostela. There was another king for Texcoco—I can't remember his name—I think it was Cacama, and the one for Iztapalapa. There were always four kings, but of them all, the one representing Tenochtitlan was the most influential."

"I see. I hadn't realized this, and I don't think I've ever heard of the existence of four kings at the same time. Please, continue."

"I'm still speaking of the procession that followed King Moctezuma. Besides those of us who belonged to his entourage, there were others who marched. There were those people who lived in the city, as well as countless others from outside who joined, knowing that the encounter with the strangers was about to happen.

"There were people on rooftops, lining the streets, crowding the squares, and overflowing the lake barges. Merchants came, as did artisans, teachers, venders, feather-makers, metal workers, lesser nobility, common soldiers, servants, slaves, women, children—all of them tightly packed, craning and stretching their necks to get at least a brief glimpse of the foreign gods.

"The women of Moctezuma's household walked behind his litter, so that what I saw was from that view. I remember only the back of the king's head and those of the rest of his companions.

"In the lead of the march went the lords of our kingdom, all dressed in the garb of their rank. Following the nobles were the eagle and jaguar warriors, and I can tell you that the number of lords and warriors was so great that I cannot now approximate a number. It must have been as impressive for the white eyes."

The woman paused and looked at Father Benito. "Are you exhausted? Would you prefer for me to skip these details?"

The monk took advantage of the moment to rub his sore hand. "No. Give whatever descriptions you can remember. I'm trying to capture it all."

"Following the nobles and warriors came King Moctezuma. He was seated in a litter which was carried by six of his peers, and escorting them were armed soldiers. The king's litter was topped by a canopy supported by four golden posts. It was carried by those lords closest to the king through family. Only they were allowed to touch him, and only they had the privilege of assisting him as he stepped down from the litter to greet Don Hernán Cortés.

"I remember most of those nobles. They are now dead, of course, but their spirits are still with us. Yes, priest, look over there, just beyond the fountain. Can you see them? They're as present today as they were upon that fateful day, and I often converse with them."

Father Benito's eyes squinted as he focused on the place pointed out by Huitzitzilin, but he saw nothing except geranium and begonia plants. When he looked back at her, he realized that her face looked strangely transfixed, and he wondered if he should end the session. But he saw her tongue moisten her lips, so he knew that she was about to speak again.

"My memory of what follows seems now like one of the paintings by your artists, the ones that hang on the walls of this convent. My meaning is that even though I can still see those people, what they wore, how they stood, and the sound of their words, it is a picture whose images are stiff and without spirit.

"When we neared the white men, the crowd opened, and I was able to see clearly. From where I stood I could see Moctezuma's back as he stepped down and stretched out his arms and the accompanying lords held his arms up."

"Stretched out his arms? Do you mean like this?" Father Benito lifted his arms simulating a bird in flight.

"Yes. It was a ritualistic practice that told everyone present that the king was like a mighty bird, its wings outstretched and ready for flight, but held down by human hands. Even though I saw only his back, I was sure that he was looking straight into the eyes of those strange pale creatures who stood gaping at us. No one spoke until the king finally uttered words that drifted back towards those of us who were closest to him.

"'Lord Feathered Serpent, I come to deliver your throne to you and to your representatives. Know that I and my ancestors have not usurped it, but rather have we guarded it for your sake. Know that we are your servants and that we are at your feet, ready to defend your honor. I know that this is not a dream; you have not come to us from the clouds and the mists of our volcanoes, but rather that you have arrived from across the reaches of the eastern ocean. Take your proper position in this land. Reign over it and its peoples as you did in the days of our ancestors.'"

The woman sat grasping her hands as she rocked back and forth in the chair. She shook her head from side to side in condemnation.

"When we heard Moctezuma say these words, we were shocked, and we looked at one another in disbelief. Our leader was handing over our kingdom to strangers when they had not even asked for it! I saw the nobles and warriors shuffle in frustration, and I wondered if they would have the courage to speak out against the king. They didn't. Instead, they held their tongue and listened to the rest of what the king had to say.

"Lifting his mantle, he bared his chest and said, 'Look, I am neither god nor monster. I am but a man who has awaited your arrival with joy and anticipation.'

"When he said this we all began to stir, momentarily confused but soon angry with Moctezuma for the ease with which he had abdicated his throne. I felt that the other kings and nobles were on the verge of dragging him away, but respect for his rank prevailed, and no one did anything while he talked even more.

"'Come, refresh yourselves. Take food and drink, for you must be fatigued after your long journey.'

"Then we heard the voice of a woman translating the king's words. I craned my neck to see who was speaking. It was she of whom we spoke, Malinche. Her slanted eyes were dark and piercing. Her mouth was wide, and her cheekbones high and broad. She had a small forehead and black, glossy hair which hung to her waist. She was dressed in white cotton, while her sandals were of iguana leather, and her jewelry, although simple, was finely wrought."

Father Benito did not write this part of Huitzitzilin's account because it was not new. He had already made a note to try to ferret out new information on the woman.

"Let me now describe Captain Cortés as I saw him for the first time. His eyes looked cold, like obsidian. They were determined and hungry like those of a coyote. Because of this I observed him closely. He was standing erect, but I saw that his legs were bowed and clad in a white material that clung to his flesh. He didn't wear sandals but coverings that concealed his feet—I wondered if they were shaped like ours.

"He was dressed in clothing made of dark material that ballooned around his hips and that reached all the way up to his neck, covering his arms down to his hands. He wore coverings on his hands, shaped to mold his fingers; this time I saw that they looked like ours. On his chest and back he wore a cage made of a material unknown to us, but it appeared to have the hardness of silver, and he had a weapon that hung upon a cincture. His headdress was round, puffy, and had a small feather stuck in it.

"His face was his most striking part, because it was colorless; it looked blanched. His eyebrows were arched and dark, and he had a bulging vein that divided his forehead. His nose was long and straight, and his mouth was round and small.

"I thought that he was ugly, but most repellent of all was the hair that covered the face of Captain Cortés as well as that of his companions. They had so much hair growing out of their faces that we gasped out loud at the sight of it, especially when we saw that the color was different on each of them. Cortés' was dark; that of others was brown, and yet on others it was golden.

"After Malinche finished speaking, there was silence while your captains stood gawking at us, their mouths hanging open. Suddenly, they moved apart and there, in front of us, were the strangest creatures ever beheld by any eyes. They were enormous beasts, four-legged and hairier yet than your captains. They snorted, puffed and clawed at the earth. We couldn't help it; we shrank back when we saw them so close.

"Suddenly, Captain Cortés approached Moctezuma, intending to embrace him, but nobles, warriors, guards, and even we women surged forward because we thought that he was going to attack the king. Cortés paled even more thinking that we were going to harm him, and he withdrew.

"After that, we all stood in silence, and that stillness has reigned in this land since then. It is the silence of our spirit, of our tongues that have dried up. It is the silence that sprang to the heavens, engulfing the winds and volcanoes, that has wrapped itself around our bodies and faces, stopping the air from entering our nostrils. It is a silence that smells of hollowness and nothingness. It is a silence of the living that are dead. It is a silence that is eternal."

Father Benito was startled by the intensity of emotion of Huitzitzilin's words. She had digressed from her description of the first encounter between the Mexicas and Spaniards, and she was instead speaking of something he did not understand but that he sensed was an assault on the presence of his people.

"What silence are you speaking of, Señora? This land is now teeming with the sounds of progress. When I leave this convent, I encounter people talking and planning. I hear the sound of new buildings in construction, of fields being prepared for the harvest. I hear the clamor of children speaking in God's language and singing His praises. What do you mean by silence?"

He halted abruptly, realizing that his voice was escalating in pitch and that he was defending a position of which he was unsure. He felt a pang of embarrassment for allowing himself to become irritated.

"You're disturbed. I see that I cannot expect you to understand what we felt at the time of that encounter. How can anyone know that we realized that the signs that had prophesied evil for our people had come true, and that it would be our generation that would see the end of our civilization.

"At that moment I understood what was happening and I began to cry. When I turned to the others for consolation, I saw that they were weeping also. Moctezuma said nothing; he merely returned to his litter. He looked like a stranger who had lived beyond his age. We all knew that it was finished. We returned to Tenochtitlan in silence."

Chapter X

"When you returned to your city, what happened? Captain Cortés has explained that you became hostile, and that he was forced to punish your people."

"That is not precise, because we did not fight him. At least not in the beginning. What happened is that we tried to live on as we had before that encounter. People went to the market place, they ate and dressed and complained and gossiped, trying to pretend nothing had happened. But it was all a lie, because we had reached our last day and we knew it. What was left of our society after that first meeting between Moctezuma and Captain Cortés was a dream, and we were the dream walkers.

"We deluded ourselves into believing that our lives would continue as before, that nothing had changed. Everyone hoped that all would be well, but we were foolish because we perished the moment our king surrendered his throne on the day I have just described. Now I know that the procession that went out to greet your captains in Iztapalapa was really a funeral cortege."

Graciela Limón

Father Benito, anxious to fill in the details of what happened during the time after the encounter, pressed Huitzitzilin. "We have been told that our men came in peace but that the Mexicas responded in bad faith, that you instead attacked slyly and in treachery."

"No! What a lie! That is not what happened!" The woman's voice rose shrilly, her words slurred against toothless gums, and her hands clutched the armrests of the chair.

"It is true that we fought back almost as soon as they arrived, but it was a struggle that happened without arms. When the king opened the gates of the city to your soldiers, treating them as if they had indeed been gods, we tried to follow his example, but soon those men began to act as if our palaces, courtyards, and market places were their own to do with as they pleased. It became clear that they thought that all they had to do was to stretch out a hand and there would be food or drink. They also took an intense liking to our women.

"We discovered almost immediately that we could no longer walk from one chamber to another without hearing a vile sound or seeing a lustful look. Our king, nevertheless, urged us to endure that humiliation, and we obeyed even though we didn't understand the reason. This went on for months before we attacked your forces, making them run and drown in the lake.

The priest stopped writing. "I thought that hostilities had begun immediately."

"No. Months passed before the battle for Tenochtitlan took place. It was then that I first became aware of him, because I felt his eyes constantly on me. He was one of the captains closest to Captain Cortés. His name was Baltazar Ovando."

Father Benito, eyebrows lifted in curiosity, cocked his head. "Captain Ovando? Who was he? I don't recall reading or hearing about him."

The woman did not avoid the monk's inquisitive gaze, but instead returned it; her expression was frank. "He became my lover."

The priest dropped the quill and reached for the stole, preparing himself for the confession he was sure to hear. He was becoming accustomed to Huitzitzilin's unpredictable turns. Suddenly, she blocked his hand in midair.

"No, priest. Not yet. I'll tell you when the time comes for you to hear the rest of my sins. In the meantime, let me speak of him a little, and then I'll continue with the details of those months previous to the death and bloodshed that led to where we are now.

"At that time I had no way of knowing whether he was handsome or not, because they all looked ugly to me. Later on, however, I grew to distinguish them and I began to see that his teeth were not rotted like those of the others, and that he did not smell as much. He was young, no more than five years older than I.

"At first, I avoided his persistent gaze, but his eyes began to entice me, luring and inviting me. I recall that he, unlike the rest of the white men, did not force himself upon me. He simply looked at me, and when finally I looked in return, I saw the gentle smile that I had seen only in Zintle's gaze. The white man's eyes were more amazing to me because they were the color of the lake's water when the sky was blue. I noticed also that his skin was the color of a white feather, and that his hair was golden, like the color of maize."

Father Benito's imagination was captivated by what the woman was saying, and he wanted to hear more. He had not expected the events of those days to be intertwined with her life, but now that she had begun to take that direction, he decided to ask her to continue.

"What about your child? And Zintle? Did Captain Ovando know about them?"

Huitzitzilin sucked her lips; the sound expressed exasperation. "I'll speak more of those matters later on. In the meantime, let me finish telling you what happened up until the fall of our city."

Benito felt the sting of embarrassment, knowing that she had noticed that he was prying. He despondently returned to recording her words.

"Moctezuma did everything in his power to please the white men. He housed them in his late father's palace, he continued to shower them with gifts, he visited them, and he even appeared to like Captain Cortés. When he had a small boat built on our lake, the king actually boarded it. They spent hours playing games of chance, or engaged in conversation. Malinche was always present because she was by that time Cortés' concubine.

"However, a truce among gods is always a short one, and so the false peace that prevailed between the captain and our king those first months broke like a fragile mirror. The pretended courtesy that marked our first encounters began to fray. Our nobles and warriors resented the ways in which your captains placed their crosses anywhere possible. We hated how our shrines were being desecrated with the presence of the lady dressed in blue, the one whose face looked small and pinched. Your monks, who were no cleaner than ours, harassed and intimidated our own priests as they arrogantly strutted in their long brown robes, dragging and rattling their wooden beads."

Father Benito stopped writing and pointed the quill at Huitzitzilin. His hand was shaking. "I shall not let you speak blasphemously about our Blessed Mother. Nor should you slander the brave missionaries who have sacrificed their lives to bring your people salvation. If you continue to do so, Señora, I will leave."

This time Huitzitzilin had gone too far, and the monk's lips quivered as he struggled with the outrage of listening to the woman as she maligned what was sacred to him. But despite his rancor, she seemed oblivious to what he had said.

"Horses and dogs defiled our courtyards, and weapons that were dragged on wheels gutted our paving. Never before had Tenochtitlan seen so much waste cast in every direction. Animal bones, unpalatable even to the dogs, were strewn over the ground. Soiled clothing, tattered foot coverings, cast-off leather, damaged and no longer useful utensils, all littered our once beautiful squares and gardens.

"We loathed the presence of your people and could not understand why Moctezuma did not put an end to it. But what most revolted us was the presence of the hateful Tlaxcaltecas, they of the rancid bread, they who aspired to our grandeur. The Tlaxcaltecas were the greatest traitors of them all!

"You ask when the real hostilities began? I'll tell you. The false truce unraveled when Captain Cortés accompanied Moctezuma to the temple of Huitzilipochtli. He demanded that the altar be wiped clean of the sacred blood that encrusted it and that a cross as well as a statue of the blue lady be installed on it. The king, for the first time, denied that command, informing the captain that Huitzilipochtli was our first lord, and that to replace him was unthinkable.

"Captain Cortés had no alternative, and so he withdrew his demand, but not with politeness. He instead scowled and turned his back on the king, an insult so glaring, so unforgivable, that news of it made its way into every corner of our city. The word went out; the gods had chilled toward one another!

"Matters became worse when news reached Tenochtitlan that our warriors had killed a Captain Juan Escalante and six of his soldiers. We all rejoiced when we received that information, because that proved to everyone that those people were not gods but men who could be defeated. Soon after, knowing that he and his followers were in danger, Captain Cortés immediately gathered his captains, and together they approached Moctezuma. That encounter was the beginning of the end. From that moment on, everyone realized that war between the Mexicas and the Whites was imminent.

"On that day, Moctezuma's wife and I were conversing with him when Captain Cortés, Malinche and his companions walked into the chamber; they came unannounced. Cortés spoke in a stiff, controlled manner, giving us the impression that underneath those words was intense anger. Malinche translated.

"'Majesty, I have cared and loved your person from the moment of our arrival. I have dealt with you in the full respect due to your honorable person, and I have done all in my power not to harm, hinder, or damage either your subjects or your city. I thought that you in turn would deal with me in like manner. But now I see that I have been deceived. You have acted dishonorably behind my back.'

"The king was not shaken, but answered in a strong voice. 'I do not know what you mean. If I, or any one of my subjects, have given you cause to say these things to me, be frank and speak directly to the meaning of your words. I have not deceived you, and your allegation that I have acted dishonorably offends me.'

"'You know what I mean!'

"The captain's voice rose in pitch, and at that moment I overheard one of the soldiers mutter 'dog!' Cortés spoke on, his face blanched, his lips glistening and trembling.

"'You know that Escalante and six of our men were murdered in a cowardly attack that took place under your orders. There is no way for you to pretend ignorance. Nothing in this land happens without your knowledge, Moctezuma!' He pronounced the king's name with disdain. 'Now we are here not to be told lies, but for you to take action to punish this crime committed against our king and our person.'

105

"There was silence in the chamber because Moctezuma refused to respond to Cortés' demand. I looked at the king's wife, but she did not betray emotion. I looked at Moctezuma and saw that his face had also turned to stone. I alone felt my body trembling.

"Then the Spaniards withdrew to one side of the chamber and conferred secretly. Suddenly, they rushed the king, surrounded him, and slapped shackles on his wrists. It happened so quickly, so unexpectedly, that his wife and I stood in stunned confusion. Moctezuma himself showed that he could not believe what was happening, and he stared at his wrists as if they were strange monsters. It all happened in a moment, but in the end Captain Cortés had transformed Moctezuma from king to prisoner.

"From there he was taken off to Cortés' chambers and kept there until the four warriors who had killed Escalante and his companions were brought to Tenochtitlan at the order of Hernán Cortés. Days after, when word spread through the city that the warriors were about to enter through the Serpent Wall, everyone abandoned what they were doing and ran out to the central square, hoping to capture a passing glimpse of those men who were by now heroes.

"They had demonstrated the courage to prove that the invaders were not gods after all. They had exerted Mexica power and prevailed against the enemy. They had single-handedly done what everyone yearned to do to the foul-smelling, vile-sounding creatures whose presence we all found sickening.

"Those warriors were now more valuable to us than perhaps our gods, because they at least were there, flesh and blood, walking and smiling, and hailing us, telling us what we could do if only we had the boldness. By that time, everyone knew of the imprisonment of Moctezuma, and knowing this threatened us more, because now we were without a leader. Nevertheless, those four Mexicas, even though held in shackles, gave us hope that somehow we would yet defeat Captain Cortés and his followers.

"The warriors marched in through the Serpent Wall holding themselves erect. Thunder could not have drowned out the roar that rose from the crowd. Nothing could have diminished the booming of the sacrificial drums that beat and pounded out their joy. Even the fire-arms of the Spaniards could not have squelched the clamor created by the thousands of rattles and the bleating of conch shells. The whooping of the war cry shattered the air, tearing at the wind.

"Despite the warriors being bound together by shackles, they were showered with gems, feathers, and flowers. Our people rushed them, pushing, thrusting, touching them, patting their shoulders and kissing them. The Spaniards looked on in gloomy silence, but we knew that they were afraid.

"Cortés silenced the clamor by stepping into the center of the square. Fists clenched and held arrogantly on his hips, he swiveled slowly in a full circle until satisfied that everyone in the crowd had seen his stony face. He turned to the prisoners and in a voice that bounced off the temple walls, he addressed them.

"'Will you confess to the murder of Captain Escalante and his men?'

"Silence. Only the sound of wind slithering from altar to altar could be heard.

"'If you recant, I will pardon you!'

"Again, there was no response, and we looked on knowing that those warriors would not do as commanded. When Cortés became convinced that they would say nothing, admit nothing, accuse no one, he gave the order.

"'Burn them!'"

Father Benito leaned back in the chair as he stared at the begonia plants. He didn't ask if the warriors had been executed because, although this incident had not been recorded nor studied in Spain, he knew enough of Captain Cortés to know that he would have indeed followed through with that punishment. Again, the priest felt torn between what he knew was justice and the growing sympathy he felt for the Indian woman's people. Disturbed, he rubbed his eyes wondering if he should put an end to the session.

"The prisoners marched to the center of the square. I was, as was my duty, accompanying the king's wife, who from the moment of his captivity hardly left his side. Then the sudden howl that went up from the crowd told us that something important was about to begin. I stepped out to the terrace and beheld a spectacle that I will never forget. In the center of the courtyard, I saw four posts with bases packed with mounds of wood.

"I stood watching as the four warriors walked with dignity and without showing fear. When my eyes focused on one of them, I realized that it was Tetla, the man whom I had hated but who was now a hero of the Mexica nation. I admit that I was shocked, and that I tried to feel sympathy, but because I could not, I concentrated on him as he was bound to the stake with ropes. There my eyes remained until his last moment.

"The people's shouting suddenly ceased, and silence engulfed us. One of the Christian priests, holding a book in his hands, muttered incantations, frequently lifted his right hand to cut the emptiness with the sign of the cross. His voice floated through the air of Tenochtitlan for all of us to hear:

"'Do you reject the Prince of Darkness and accept the Prince of Light? Do you disdain your life of sin and take to your bosom the true God? Do you forsake the infernal realm of Satan and yearn for paradise?'

"There was no response to the priest's questions, only silence.

"'Do you reject your idols and embrace the loving kindness of He who is pure mercy? Do you reject your evil ways and solemnly promise to follow the way of virtue? Do you repudiate the fiendish ways of your ancestors and take to your heart the chastising light of the cross?'

"Again, nothing happened. Not a sound came from the warriors that awaited death. There was silence in the courtyard of Tenochtitlan. Only a cold, tired wind blew from the summits of the volcanoes. The priest looked around him, blinking, showing that he was baffled and that he did not know what to do.

"For a moment he turned toward the prisoners in a supplicating way. Then his body changed, stiffened, his face grew red, and in a loud voice he shouted, 'Then I condemn you and your foul idols to the bowels of hell, and to the eternal flames of Lucifer and his legion of demons, there to be purified and tortured for ages upon ages. Amen!'

"'Amen!' the voices of the Spaniards echoed the word, but their expression sounded thin and uncertain. Then the fire was lighted at each of the men's feet.

"Señora, I witnessed such acts of purification when I was a boy, and I need not record such a description. Besides, Holy Mother Church has carefully chronicled these events which are well known to our scholars. It brings nothing new."

Huitzitzilin ignored Benito's words and went on speaking. "The billows of smoke rose to the height of the Great Temple. The cackle of branches sputtered and soon flames engulfed the bodies of the men. I could not remove my eyes from Tetla's body; that body that had abused my own, that had caused me pain and humiliation. I watched his face and, except for the twitching of the muscles around his lips, it was as calm as it had been upon the day of our wedding.

"Sweat began to pour from his face and body as the tongues of fire licked first at his ankles and knees and thighs, then at his stomach and chest, then his neck, throat, and face. His hair caught fire and exploded into a mass of flame that danced upward, elongating him, giving him a height he had never possessed. Soon he was wrapped in blue and purple flames. I could no longer distinguish his body from the glare, and so what had been brown flesh was now a snarl of red and gold and black.

"Then Tetla began to dissolve! His flesh became liquid; it dripped unevenly, running off his body in globs. I saw his body quiver, but yet no sound came from his mouth. What had once had been Tetla became smaller, shorter, reduced first to the shortness of a stalk of maize, then to the size of those dwarfs who entertained Moctezuma, then smaller still to the size of a low chair, until there remained only a head that soon became obscured by swirling ash and thick gray smoke.

"Tetla was dead, and I am a witness that he never uttered a cry of pain. In Tenochtitlan, silence reigned like an evil scourge after that execution, and if anyone listened carefully, all that could be heard was the weeping of Moctezuma, king of the once mighty Mexica nation."

Chapter XI

Father Benito was late that morning, and when he entered the cloister he found that Huitzitzilin was not waiting for him in the usual place. He looked around, squinting his eyes against the morning sunlight until he finally saw her strolling through the shadows cast by the stone pillars.

Before he cut across the garden to join her, he took his time watching her; she seemed to be speaking to someone. After a while he saw that he had been right; she was talking. He could hear her high-pitched voice, that lilt that transformed what she was saying into song. When he concentrated on her words, the monk realized that it was not Spanish; she was speaking in her native tongue.

"Buenos días, Señora. I apologize for being late," Benito called out to the woman from across the garden.

"Good morning, priest." She stopped where she was, responding to him as she raised her hands. She waited for him to pick his way through the potted plants and around the fountain until he reached her.

"Shall we return to our chairs?" He smiled broadly at her as he held on to the leather bag.

"In a minute. Let us stroll for a while longer. It's when I walk that I'm able to better speak with those that have gone before me."

Benito, walking alongside the woman, cocked his head quizzically. He had heard her say before that she often spoke with people who had died, but he had not given it much thought.

"That's as it should be, Señora. Holy Mother Church requires us to pray for the souls in purgatory."

Huitzitzilin stopped where she was and looked up at Benito's face. Her gaze was intense as she held her head in a way that hid the scarred socket.

"Our spirits never leave us to go to that place you mentioned. They stay here with us, and because of that we don't pray for them. Instead, we speak with them."

The woman gestured with both hands, showing Benito that the souls of her people surrounded them. "There on that branch is Moctezuma; his spirit clings to it. And over there, seated by the fountain, is Zintle. And look! Right behind you..."

The woman suddenly jerked her arm upward as her finger pointed, making Benito jump. He instinctively spun around, expecting to see a feathered warrior or even the burning Tetla, whose image had awakened the priest several times during the night. But he saw nothing, only the shimmering autumn air, and he chuckled inwardly, deriding himself for being so foolish. He had actually expected to see a ghost. He sighed deeply, knowing that it was from relief.

"As you say, but I would like us to begin working soon because of my lateness this morning."

"Did somebody die?"

"On the contrary, three new brothers arrived from home last night and we had a mass of thanksgiving this morning. It went on longer than expected."

"Ah!" Huitzitzilin didn't say anything but turned toward the nook where her chair was placed. Father Benito followed her, walking at her slow pace and anticipating what she would relate to him on that day. He was so taken with what he was thinking that he bumped into her when she stopped abruptly.

"It was during those months of waiting that in my jealousy and loneliness I listened to the demon of lust."

Father Benito was startled by her words; as usual when speaking of her sins, the words were unexpected. He had prepared himself to hear more of the events leading to the fall of Tenochtitlan, and now she was telling of something that surely must have trapped her into transgression.

"Lust? That should be mentioned only in confession, Señora. Is that what you want? Do you want me to hear your sins instead of what you were speaking about yesterday?"

"I cannot separate one from the other. These things happened in my life at the same time, one causing the other, and that intertwining with something else. Oh, please don't reach for your mantle." She stopped his arm as he began looking for the stole in his pocket. "Can't you just listen to me, then decide what must be forgiven and what must be written?"

Benito frowned but led the way to their place in silence because inwardly he had already accepted what she asked. When she settled in the chair, she began to speak, and the priest listened, his arms resting on his knees.

"Zintle married another woman during those days. There were many such unions then. I suppose it made us all believe that such things would help us against the enemy. As for me, it caused me jealousy, and in my bitterness I took refuge in Baltazar Ovando. Do you remember that I mentioned him before? He was one of the captains that had entered Tenochtitlan.

"You have wondered about my son and how I could have betrayed him by joining my body to that of the enemy. I cannot explain it to you, but I will tell you that I abandoned myself to the torture of jealousy, and when I sensed the blue eyes of the white man upon me, I responded to the wicked spirit of lust, hoping to find relief.

"Little was needed to arouse me, and when he approached me, I didn't hesitate. I fornicated with him many times. I put aside the truth that he was the enemy. I forgot that I loved Zintle and that I had a child. I forgot myself as well, and I could think only of the intense urge that prompted me toward that white body covered with golden fur."

Huitzitzilin looked at Father Benito, whose face was buried in his hands. He was hunched over; she could see the redness that was tinting his neck. When she stopped speaking, he remained in that position, as if he hadn't heard that she was finished.

"Are you ill, priest?"

"No. I'm not. But what you're telling me should be uttered only in confession, don't you understand?" His voice was filled with frustration and irritation.

"I see. Then I'll return to the events of the city. But please remember that I will come back to this part of my life because it is connected with other things that happened to me.

"Shortly after Tetla's death, life in Tenochtitlan appeared to return to its normal pace. Captain Cortés removed the shackles from Moctezuma's wrists and ankles and tried to renew the relationship they had before the executions. The king, however, did not respond; he was morose one day, sad the next. I remained close to his wife, and it was at that time that I began to spend more and more time with Captain Baltazar."

Father Benito had resumed writing what Huitzitzilin had to say, intent on recording every one of her words. Whenever he fell behind, he asked her to repeat the omitted word or phrase. She, in turn, had transported her spirit back to those days before the fall of Tenochtitlan.

"I say that things appeared to be as before, but that was not true. We all were aware of the stiffness that marked our talk and our actions, even the most trivial or ordinary. Moctezuma's council ceased to visit him. The nobles and warriors were also absent, and they did this without leave. The wives and concubines of our king disappeared, with the exception of my mistress. His jesters and entertainers came and went as they pleased, and even the quality of his food began to worsen. It was obvious that Moctezuma was losing the respect of the people.

"Even the everyday activity of the city was affected. Traffic in the canals and streets dwindled to a trickle. Noises became muffled, and the usually heavy flow of news from other parts of the kingdom nearly stopped.

"Soon after, Baltazar was selected as one of the officers to accompany Captain Cortés on a trip to the eastern coast, where a certain Captain Narváez was causing trouble. It was rumored that Cortés was apprehensive of whatever mischief that man might cause behind his back.

"By that time Moctezuma's spirit had almost broken down. He neither spoke nor looked anyone in the face. We were barely able to force food into his mouth, and his body seemed to be shrinking.

"He was in that condition when his council finally decided to take action, and they came to inform him of what was happening. They claimed that the War God had appeared to several people, commoners and nobles, demanding that Moctezuma cast out the white devils. The Feathered One was incensed, they said, especially with the desecration of his temples. He protested that the golden ornaments that had been dedicated to his honor now had been melted into bricks in sacrilege."

Huitzitzilin stopped speaking, allowing time for Father Benito to write what she had just said. But her pause lingered as if she were waiting for him to speak. "Aren't you interested in what the Feathered God was demanding?"

"I don't think it was a god or any such thing that was complaining. What I think is that the people under your king realized that strong action had to be taken, else the end of the kingdom would take place, which, of course, is what happened."

"Yes. They were looking for a way to be honest with the king. Almost without waiting for Moctezuma to speak about the god, the spokesmen admitted to the king that several of them had taken steps even without his approval. They had sent gifts to bribe Captain Narváez, hoping to turn him against Cortés and create ill will among the white men. They were certain that this would give the Mexicas time to prepare an attack on the Spanish captains.

"His reaction was strange, though. Instead of feeling encouraged by what his nobles had done, Moctezuma became more dejected after that meeting. Some days he was so still that we were certain that he had died."

Benito interrupted his writing. "Was he a coward? Why did he react that way?"

"Many have said as much, but it is not true. He was trapped, you see, caught between the opposing demands of two gods, and he didn't know how to resolve the dilemma. He could not find a way of balancing one divinity against the other."

"How do you know all of this? No one has ever written or spoken of these matters."

"I was there, close to him, and I saw with my eyes, and heard with my ears what I'm telling you."

"But Captain Cortés has written that your people felt betrayed by Moctezuma."

"How would he have known? I've told you that he left the city in search of Narváez. He wasn't even in the city at the time, so anything that he said about what happened he heard from someone else."

Benito was silent for a while, thinking, "There was talk of a massacre that took place in his absence. Did it really happen?"

"Yes. Captain Alvarado was put in charge, and when Cortés left, our spirits rose because we saw it as the opportunity to cast out the white soldiers that remained in the city. Under the pretense of a celebration, our leaders chose the day during which the Spaniards would be surprised and killed. On that day, word spread from mouth to mouth. 'Dress in your finest. Report to the temple courtyard where weapons will be supplied. Be alert. Kill until the last of the intruders is dead.'

"That day was even more fatal than expected because unknown to anyone, a Tlaxcalteca spy discovered our plan and revealed it to Captain Alvarado, and when the people met in the courtyard, the white soldiers were ready and waiting for us. With one stroke the Spaniards put down hundreds of our people."

Huitzitzilin was so moved by her recollections that she had to stop speaking, and she held her hands in her lap as the memory of that day swept over her. Father Benito was captivated by the unheard of description of that day, but though he wanted her to continue, he kept silent. He knew the outcome of those events, but now, in his heart, he would have wanted the woman's world not to have been destroyed.

"As planned, every available warrior presented himself at the temple. Women and children would not have been there under normal conditions, but that day was different. Women, along with their children, became partners with men in the first battle between us and the white invaders.

"The courtyard filled with people. At first glance the crowd appeared festive, happy, and noisy. We all wore our most beautiful gowns, mantels, feathered headdresses, gems, golden broaches, and earplugs. But if anyone looked closely, it would have been noticed that the men wore mantles which hid breast shields and war girdles. It would have been clear that our faces did not really smile. Instead, eyes signaled one another, and there was a strain in our greetings. These were the signs that told of the real motive for that gathering.

"As with all of our great ceremonies, it was to begin with the dance of the Serpent Goddess, Cihuatcoatl, and I was one of the women who were invited to be a witness along with other noble women. We stood at the corner of the main court, where the church now stands."

"Just a moment. Do you remember which corner?" Benito felt himself transported to that day.

"As you face the church, it would have been the corner which is to your right side. It was from there that I could see what was happening. Once when I looked upward, I thought I saw the silhouette of a soldier who seemed to be watching. My fear began at that moment. What was he doing there? Were there others? Had we not been given permission to celebrate this day? What if they knew of our intentions? Despite these questions, I persuaded myself that all was well.

"Boom! Boom! Boom! The giant snake drum belched its deep, hollow voice. Boom! Boom! Boom! We heard the voice of the drum that had been silent ever since the death of our four noble warriors. Boom! Boom! Boom!"

Father Benito's hand flew across the parchment, trying to keep up with what he was hearing. His face was flushed with the excitement caused by the vivid description, and he even included the sounds that came out of Huitzitzilin's pursed lips in imitation of the legendary drum that only the first discoverers got to see.

"HaaaReee! HaaaReee! The ceremonial conch shells bleated their mournful cry as we prepared for the ceremonies in honor of the War God which were to be led by his priests. That was the last time such a dance was enacted. It was the final tribute to a god whose days were numbered, because even though later on many of your captains and soldiers were immolated in the god's honor, never again did his priests adore him and pay him homage as they did on that final day.

"The beat of smaller drums, accompanied by flutes, began the priests' dance, as well as that of the people, for we too participated by just standing in one place. The accompanying rhythm of gourds worn by the priests around their ankles and wrists announced their entrance into the courtyard through the portals in the Snake Wall. Led by the High Priest, they slid and slithered in, keeping rhythm with naked feet, with rattles shaking and drums thump-thumping, increasing and intensifying their beat. All of us moved with the throbbing sound of the drums and flutes and the heavy humming that was emitted from the throats of the priests.

"Hummmm! Hummmm! Hummmm! It was a dark, deep voice that came from many breasts, its doleful sound seizing and entangling our spirit so that we swayed and swung as would a serpent's body, becoming more and more transported and enraptured by the divine voice. Hummmm! The sound created music that flowed from throats smeared with holy blood and saturated with peyote and mescal.

"The priests reached the center of the courtyard. They were dressed in black robes, and their ears, torn in tribute to Huitzilipochtli, dripped blood that trickled to their feet. They formed a circle and there they began the dance.

"Their feet stamped; their rattles clamored. Each priest raised a clenched hand which held the sharp obsidian knife of the sacrifice, and with it he slashed at the billows of burning copal incense. They swayed, and we swayed. They hummed, and we hummed. Their eyes rolled back into their heads so that only the white balls shone, and we did the same thing. Their heads were thrust back and their long, blood-coagulated hair grazed the ground. We did likewise. With open mouths and blackened tongues that were stiff and thrust outward, our priests danced, their shoulders tracing a sensuous up and down curve.

"Then the spirit of Huitzilipochtli sprang from the underbelly of the world, hissing and snaking its way through the priests' throats, out through their gaping mouths. They all uttered the words, but only one voice resounded the growling curse of the War God.

"We entered ecstasy as we were transported to the kingdom of the dead. There we swayed and swerved. Bent backward as far as possible, sweating and panting, we sang in tribute to the god who had made us. We descended to the land of the dead, and from there upward to the thirteenth heaven.

"Rattles rattling, drums pounding, voices hissing and humming and chanting, feet sliding on the pavement stones, bodies swaying in rapture; thus did we, the Mexica people, pay final homage to our god of gods in the twilight of his time."

Father Benito, quill held in midair, realized that he was holding his breath. When he felt a sharp pain hit between his eyebrows, he let out a long, hollow sigh. His imagination had taken him to that day described by Huitzitzilin. His heart was beating, and he felt aroused; his body tingled, and he could not control or make it obey him. His face was flushed as he gawked at the Indian woman.

"They were indeed sorcerers. Nothing less than that, and they must have been in league with Satan himself!" he blurted out.

"Why? Because they have touched you even after so many years have passed since their extinction?"

Unnerved by the woman's words, Father Benito hastily gathered his writing materials and stuffed them into the leather bag; he felt his hands trembling. Without a word he walked away, taking long strides. Before leaving the cloister, he turned to look at the woman; he saw that she was staring at him. He shook his head in bewilderment.

Chapter XII

"The woman said that one voice sounded through the throats of the scoundrels who called themselves priests. One voice, Father Anselmo! One horrible sound that belched out commands for the sacrifice of our soldiers."

Father Benito was seated in front of his superior. They were again in the monastery library; it was night. Listening to the young priest, Anselmo sat rigidly in the wooden chair while he distractedly fingered its bronze rivets. He remained silent, not wanting to interrupt.

"It cannot be anything other than sorcery, don't you agree?" Benito's voice was unsteady.

"Or trickery."

The young man's eyes widened as he discerned a skeptical look in the monk's steady gaze. He recalled their conversation of a few days before, when Anselmo had cautioned him to beware of sorcery, of hexes, of the power of these people to conjure evil spirits. Now he seemed to be making a round-about turn in introducing the element of trickery in the place of witchcraft.

Benito readjusted himself in the chair and cleared his throat while he dealt with the surprise caused by this new possibility. "Then, you don't think that it was the work of Satan?"

"Oh, I didn't say that, Brother. I'm simply allowing room for doubt. We know that the people of this land were indeed in league with the devil; the worshipping of idols, the shedding of human blood as well as their cannibalistic practices, give ample grounds to believe it. On the other hand..." Anselmo's voice trailed, causing Father Benito even more travail and confusion regarding the prior's frame of mind.

"On the other hand, what?"

"On the other hand, it could be that the old woman is deceiving you, playing with your imagination. Ask yourself if you have ever heard of such a foolish dance performed by men. Oh, we know that Satan exists and that he held the tribe of this city in his grip. But the early explorers did not describe rituals such as the ones described by your sly old woman, and that must have been because they never happened. What our captains did record were those acts of butchery that proved that the people of this city were indeed pawns of the devil."

Benito slouched back in the hard chair, making its leather creak. The thought that Huitzitzilin was deliberately lying angered him. Yet he knew that Anselmo was right, because nothing that the younger monk had ever read or heard came close to what the woman described that day.

Stiff, blackened tongues! Rolling white eyeballs! Backs bent backward as far as possible! A roaring voice from the entrails of the earth! And everything under the watchful eyes of Captain Alvarado! If such a dance had indeed taken place, certainly he would have written about it. These thoughts made the monk suddenly sit up rigidly, convinced that the Indian woman was feeding him tales and making fun of him.

"You must be on your guard." Father Anselmo leaned forward as he whispered his final advice to Benito. "Don't eat or drink anything that she offers you. Keep your distance while you transcribe what she says. Don't allow her to seduce you into believing that her ways were in any manner proper or virtuous. And above all, Brother, don't let her make a fool of you by feeding you far-fetched falsehoods invented by her old brain. Don't fall into the trap of trusting her merely because she is aged. Remember the saying that affirms that Satan knows so much not because he is the devil, but because he is old."

Chapter XIII

Father Benito had prayed longer the previous night waiting for his anger to pass away and, even though it did abate, he still felt its sting when he faced Huitzitzilin the next morning. Without greeting her, he cleared his voice, seated himself farther away than usual, and sat waiting to write what she had to say. She noticed this and frowned.

"Why are you so far away from me this morning?"

"Am I?"

The monk's voice was cold, and after a few moments he scooted the chair a few inches towards the woman, but his discomfort was now more evident.

"What is the matter?"

"To be frank, I shall ask you to refrain from exaggerating the events you remember, and limit your words to only those things that did happen."

"I have not exaggerated anything. Everything is as it happened, as I saw it! It is not my fault if it contradicts what you have been taught."

They remained quiet; only the chirping of the birds and the gurgling sounds of water in the fountain broke the silence.

"Do you want me to continue?"

"Yes."

"Good!" Huitzitzilin inhaled deeply, held her breath, then slowly exhaled. "The spell into which our dancing had cast us that day was broken by an explosion."

Huitzitzilin began her narrative at the point at which she had left off the day before. Father Benito had to shuffle through his papers to find the last page.

"In our reverie we had not taken notice that the doors of the Snake Wall had been closed and that fire-belching sticks had been aimed in our direction. In our rapture we had not seen the white soldiers and their Tlaxcalteca allies take position to attack us. The blast that brought us back was the firing of those weapons. The first burst cut down many of our people.

"Shock gripped us! It was not as we had planned! Fear leaped from person to person. Mothers rushed to shield children; men attempted to reach their weapons. We scattered throughout the courtyard in waves, like water splashing from one side of a gourd to the other. We shrieked, we moaned, and the detonations would not stop. Blood began to drip, then to smear, then to over-flow on the courtyard stones. When the enemy no longer could use their fire-vomiting rods, they jumped in among the people and began to lance and cut and pry with their sharpened axes and swords. We were defenseless. We were unable to reach the intended weapons and had nothing but our hands with which to protect ourselves."

Father Benito regained confidence because here was
an event that he knew had indeed occurred. The chronicles attested to the fact that the Mexicas had been surprised in a conspiracy against the few Spanish soldiers
who had remained in Tenochtitlan. It had been a clear
attempt to destroy the white men, but the Spaniards
had acted quickly and successfully in foiling the plot.
This was safe ground for the monk, and he gladly took in
what the woman had to say about her part in that
attempted rebellion.

"I was knocked backward and dragged by the mass
of people struggling to reach a door, a crevice, anything
that could provide shelter. Several bodies fell on me. The
noise of screaming voices became intolerable. The stench
of blood, smoke, urine, and excrement was sickening. I
was choking; tears blinded my eyes and mucus flowed
from my nose, melting with the sweat of my body.

"I heard a voice screaming so horribly that I was
shaken back to clarity. That voice was mine! I was howl-
ing like a beast that knew not what to do, where to go. I
screeched like the night owl. My tongue hung out of my
mouth; I could not control it. Yet the enemy continued to
hack and cut. They ran after anything that moved,
thrusting their weapons in every direction They shouted; their faces looked monstrous to me. I saw flaccid lips
smeared with saliva that dripped over beards. Blue eyes
bulged. I saw blotchy skin distorted by fear and hatred.

"The entrails of our people curled around the soldiers' boots, limbs dangled from their pikes, and they
continued to attack because in their fear they had lost
control over themselves. Their arms could not cease

slashing. Their legs could not stop trampling. They bayed like coyotes, they wheezed like vultures, and finally when they saw that all was finished, they plundered the bodies and parts of bodies.

"They filled their pockets with anything that was gold: earplugs, necklaces, ankle and wrist braces, headbands, and broaches. The greedy white men stole everything they could, loading themselves so that they could hardly walk."

Benito's anger returned because he was certain that she was intentionally exaggerating the details. Most of all, he resented her portrayal of the Spaniards as greedy beasts.

"Why are you making it sound as if the Mexicas were innocent and unjustly treated? Were they not planning to do the same thing to the Spaniards? If those soldiers did what they did that day, it was in self-defense."

"Including plundering? Including hacking children to pieces?" The woman's voice vibrated with outrage as she responded to the monk's remarks. He didn't answer because he felt himself on the verge of walking away from her, never to return. His silence, however, encouraged her to go on.

"When the surge of people knocked me down, I remained pinned under the weight of bodies, but I could see everything. Each of the details that I have given this record was seen by my eyes, and even though I lived, at that moment I wished that I had died."

Benito looked at the woman with an expression that told her that he didn't feel sympathy. His face was stamped with a look of skepticism, and he raised his eyebrows suspiciously.

"How is it possible that you remember so many details with so much precision? These events took place more than sixty years ago."

"I remember because those happenings were burned into my memory. I'm sure that even your captains, those that are still alive, remember just as clearly."

Father Benito put down the quill and began massaging his knuckles. He wanted to cut down on the woman's brutal descriptions and instead fill his pages with more of the personal confrontation between Spaniards and Mexicas.

"Can you describe Moctezuma's death?"

"Yes, but aren't you interested in what happened after the killings I've just described?"

"Yes, but not in so much detail. I would rather have you tell about the king's death."

Huitzitzilin took a deep breath and exhaled slowly; the air wheezed through her withered nostrils. She nodded her head in agreement.

"Captain Cortés returned to Tenochtitlan and to war because after the massacre, our people armed themselves, deciding to die rather than to be slaves."

"Tell me about the king's death."

"Yes! Yes! I'm getting there! As I've already told you, I kept the king's wife company and we were usually in his chamber. I remember that when he returned, Cortés realized that the Mexicas intended to kill him, so with his men, he barged in on Moctezuma, still thinking that the king held power over his people. The usually blue vein on Cortés' forehead looked black and bulging, and his cheeks quivered. His stiffened arms were partially outstretched, and his fingers clenched and unclenched. It was apparent that he feared for his life.

"Without speaking to any of us, he and his soldiers rushed to the king and took hold of him. Those of us present tried to help him, but it was useless because we were mostly women. Cortés and Alvarado took Moctezuma, forcing him to the terrace where he could be seen by people massed in the courtyard. This all happened very quickly and without explanations.

"Then the silence that had up to that moment prevailed in our city turned to a roar. Drums, conch shells and rattles combined with voices demanding the blood of the white men. I saw Captain Cortés raise his trembling arm high into the air. The clamor ceased! All the while Moctezuma remained motionless.

"There was silence. The wind sighed as it slid off the volcanoes, and only the sound of shuffling feet broke the stillness. I will say here that no one shouted or insulted Moctezuma as some have claimed. How many times have I overheard others say that it was Cuauhtémoc who called the king a woman of the Spaniards, and that as a result he was killed by a rock cast by one of our people."

"One moment, please! We all know that Moctezuma was indeed assassinated by his own people." Benito had stopped writing.

"That is not true! Some would like to believe it happened that way, but it did not."

"Señora, why would anyone want to distort the truth? What gain would come of it?"

Huitzitzilin's face was taut, her lips were thinner than usual. "The murder of a king by his own people is an evil deed, one that proves their corruption. If the Mexicas had betrayed what was most sacred to them, then that would be proof of their vileness, and their destruction would be thus justified. What would be the gain, you ask? Not what, I respond, but who? To that question I answer that it was your people who gained by such a lie.

"Here is how it happened. When Moctezuma stepped into full view of his people, he was met with silence because everyone was shocked by his appearance. By that time he had deteriorated beyond belief. His limbs had withered and his shoulders were slumped. His face was drawn and lined with countless wrinkles. His mouth was a thin outline of what it had once been. His eyes were hollow sockets; their fire was extinguished. All that could be seen in him was grief. His hair hung limp and slicked against his skull.

"In truth, no one spoke! Cortés turned his head from the people, then to those of us on the terrace, then again to the people. It appeared that he wanted to say something either to us or to the masses, because his mouth opened and shut repeatedly.

"When our people realized that Moctezuma was nearing death, their screaming began. It was then that Cortés lost courage and suddenly withdrew back into the chamber. Once inside, he turned to his captains and through clenched teeth muttered, 'Take care of this dog!'

"No! This is another of your inventions!" Father Benito challenged the woman with a raised hand and finger that nearly grazed the tip of her nose. "Everyone knows that Captain Cortés never gave such an order!"

"Oh, but he did. I was present. I heard it with my own ears."

"You're lying!"

Getting to his feet, Father Benito began to walk away from Huitzitzilin, but something held him back. A thought flashed through his mind, suggesting that what she had said was not impossible. Cortés was known for having made several shocking decisions.

The priest stopped where he was, mulling over this possibility and the impact that it might have on his document. He turned on his heels and found the woman's uplifted face; she was gazing at him. Her expression told him that she knew his thoughts, but he returned to the chair anyway.

"When Cortés left the chamber, three of his captains remained. One of them was Baltazar Ovando. They had their orders, and those of us who had remained in the room knew what was going to happen. Moctezuma's wife tried to shield her husband, but one of the Spaniards hit her on the head and she died instantly. When I lunged forward to help her, the same man swung out but missed my face. Baltazar and the other man forced me aside, and when my eyes met those of the man with whom I had lain, he said nothing. He only stared back at me with vacant eyes.

"It was Baltazar who took hold of Moctezuma and dragged him across the floor to a corner where he pulled his dagger and plunged it into the king's neck, chest, and stomach. Moctezuma remained silent; the only sound came from the mashing of the knife against his flesh.

"Despite Baltazar lowering his head, I saw the murderer's face. It was distorted with rage and madness; it was repulsive beyond all words. The face that I had found beautiful was now hideous. The expression that I had thought gentle became monstrous.

"When it was finished, Baltazar and the others left the chamber. They didn't bother with me, nor with the bodies of the king and his wife. I remained curled on the floor because I didn't have the strength to move. I don't know how long I stayed that way. A short time later, I was roused by the frightened voices of servants who had come to see what had happened. I got to my feet, trying to shake off the terror that gripped me and to order them to help me with the bodies.

"They ran! Like rabbits, they scurried. Except for one, they all escaped, but even he refused to help me. Then I struck his face. I hit him many times, but still he cowered, inciting me to beat him until blood dripped from his ears and nose. Then he sprang to his feet and ran away.

"I was alone, but I knew that the king's body had to be treated with reverence. Leaving his wife behind, I struggled with him until I reached an isolated corner of the palace, rubbed his body with oil, and then set it on fire.

"In the beginning, the body burned slowly, then with more energy until it was reduced to ashes. Our people were now waging war on the Spaniards. No one took time to investigate the reason for fire and smoke within the confines of the palace. When it was finished, I scraped the ashes into a pot and buried it in one of the palace walls. All of this happened on the same night during which the Spaniards were driven from our city. The Sad Night, as it is now known to your people."

Father Benito put down the quill and rubbed his eyebrows several times as if trying to smooth over ideas that were crashing inside his mind. Had the captains truly assassinated Moctezuma? If so, the chronicles and letters held by the Spanish crown either lied on this point or were deceived.

The priest stared at the woman for several minutes, trying to detect signs that might indict her of having lied, but he saw none. Her body appeared calm as did her face. She seemed relieved, as if she had rid herself of a weight long buried in her memory.

Benito carefully arranged his documents in the pouch. He cleaned the tip of the quill and put it in its place. When he tied the leather tongs, he patted the bag and looked at Huitzitzilin's face. Then he got to his feet. Before leaving he said, "Perhaps it did happen as you say it did."

Chapter XIV

"When the people of Tenochtitlan drove away the white soldiers and the tribes that had helped them, they returned to their homes to celebrate their deliverance. Several of the enemy had been captured. They were offered in tribute to Huitzilipochtli almost immediately."

Huitzitzilin had resumed her story. Father Benito, increasingly less intimidated by the mention of that god, put aside Father Anselmo's warning against its mention. He justified this by reminding himself that this information was already widely known in Spain and hardly considered heresy. The priest remembered that it had been Cortés himself who had conveyed the horror felt by him and the soldiers who had survived that ordeal, when they actually had seen their comrades being sacrificed.

"But you've only mentioned those days in passing. Don't you have any recollections of it?"

"Yes, I remember as if it had happened yesterday. When the Mexica saw what had become of their king, they declared a holy war against the white men. The first thing that was done was the removal of bridges inside the city, thus trapping the enemy. It all happened so fast that the snare had been laid for the Spaniards by the time I finished with Moctezuma's ashes.

"Several days passed during which our people attacked the Spaniards with arrows and lances, or whatever else could do harm. The white men fought back with fire-spitting weapons, but they were overwhelmed by our numbers. Soon they, their allies and their animals were without fresh water or food, and eventually, in the silence of night, we could hear their groaning. After a while, we heard even their whimpering.

"It took eight days for Captain Cortés to devise a plan to escape the trap. In that time he designed a wooden bridge that could be carried by hand and used to cross the canals connecting the causeways out of the city. His men were able to construct the bridge using materials ripped out of the palaces where they were living. When they were finished, the captain gave the order to evacuate Tenochtitlan during night time. It was a rainy night, I remember."

"The captain's account tells that the escape took place during the last night of June. However, he isn't clear as to what went wrong." Father Benito spoke quietly as he recalled the information sent by Cortés to the King of Spain.

"The plan went wrong when one of our women happened to see the Spaniards sneaking out of the city. She began to shout, alerting those around her, and from there the entire city. At that moment, the Sad Night began for the white intruders.

"A woman! How ironic."

"Priest, don't be surprised. Mexica women were important throughout those days. We faced the ordeal in equal measure with the warriors. We were involved, many times even during battle, and most certainly during the last siege."

Father Benito reflected on what Huitzitzilin said. It was logical that Cortés should have omitted this in his reports. He had glossed over the fact that regional tribes had been crucial to his victory over the Mexicas, as he had also done regarding his own soldiers, claiming most of the credit for himself. The priest saw that the captain would not want to mention the role of native women in the event which turned out to be his greatest humiliation.

"Then what happened, Señora?"

"HaaReee! HaaReee!"

Without warning, Huitzitzilin let out the Mexica war whoop. Her voice was so loud and shrill that it startled Father Benito, making his arm jerk, nearly toppling the ink pot. He looked at her, amazed that she had such power in her lungs. Then he looked around, wondering why no one in the convent had come to see what was happening.

"The call to war and to what our people had been awaiting was sounded, and all of us—men, women, and even children—rose in jubilation, knowing that since it was decreed that we were to be the last of our nation, then at least it would be our joy to be the ones to plunge our knives into those pale breasts. Ours would be the honor to offer their hearts to Huitzilipochtli."

Benito's eyes narrowed in disbelief. He looked at Huitzitzilin and saw a frail, old woman who was admitting her part in the sacrifice of his countrymen. When she saw the look of horror on his face, she changed.

"I've shocked you again. I'll go on, but I'll mention only those details that caused the Spaniards to be killed or cast out of our city. Nothing more.

"As they were attempting to leave, it began to rain heavily. Their vision was impeded. They slipped and fell under their four-legged beasts. Sheets of water poured down on them. In the darkness, those crawling, creeping men looked like squirming worms. Amid the booming of the Snake Drum, the din and clash of metal and wood, the screeching of animals, our warriors rushed the escaping horde from behind, as well as from the lake, where countless canoes stabbed their flanks. All the while, the Spaniards were pounded by arrows and lances.

"We women took places on rooftops, casting stones and pointed objects on their heads. All the while we whooped and screamed like devils, knowing that the pandemonium would increase their fear. Cortés and his captains were able to cross the causeways leading to the edge of the lake, but since they had only one bridge for the entire army, our warriors did not give them time to cross. The trap closed.

"When Captain Cortés turned to look back, he saw a snarl of armor, horses, and lances. He saw men jumping one on top of the other, trying to make their way across the bridge. He saw many of them fall into the lake and sink like floundering turtles dragged down by the weight of stolen treasure. He saw Captain Alvarado sink his lance into a dead body, bracing himself forward to safety. He saw his concubine rushing over human limbs, stepping on heads and shoulders so that she could live. Then it suddenly ended."

Father Benito shook his head from side to side. "One account says that when the captain turned back and saw what you have described, he broke down and wept like a child. The tree under which he cried is still there. It was among the first things that I was shown when I arrived here."

"I'm sure you were shown a tree, but I doubt that the captain wept."

"You doubt it? Why?"

"Because jackals do not cry."

Chapter XV

"It was a mistake." Huitzitzilin went on reflecting on the days that ended with the Sad Night.

"What was a mistake?"

"Not to follow our enemies that night to exterminate them. But at the time we were so jubilant, so filled with joy and relief that we had rid our city of the invader, that all we could think of doing was to turn to Huitzilipochtli. Our new leaders, Cuitlahuac and Cuauhtémoc, had gained our confidence. Their war tactics had proven effective, and we as a people had need to raise our spirits once again.

"We returned to our temples, but we were wrong. By doing that, the Mexicas allowed Cortés to retreat, gather more tribes as allies, gain time to recuperate strength, and then attack again. But then, I'm certain that all of that has been recorded in your documents, has it not?"

"Yes, it has."

"Let me ask you this. How were the Mexicas really defeated?"

Father Benito looked at the woman, not knowing exactly what her question meant. For a moment he thought that she might be trying to fool him, and he smiled, but it was forced.

"The tribe was defeated by the superior soldiering led by Captain Cortés in the final battle for Tenochtitlan." The priest heard his words and realized that they sounded hollow. They were repetitions of what he had been told since childhood.

"That's what the chronicles say, but it was not truly that way. Before Captain Cortés returned to avenge his honor, we were cut down by the most horrible thing that had ever struck our people. It was more cruel than the starvation and thirst we suffered when we were later put under siege. It was the disease brought to us by your soldiers, and it became more terrifying than your weapons. It was more frightening than your dogs, and it was a death more painful than the tortures inflicted on us by the new Spanish masters.

"It was the pestilence! The walking terror struck this land with unimaginable force, unleashing the white man's madness on our people. It was worse than the killings at the temple, because we could not see the enemy. A mother could not raise her fist against the purple demon. A man was incapable of using his shield or knife. A king could not send out his army to have the killer extinguished. The black death was invisible, its bald head unseen, its grinning teeth beyond our vision.

"We had expelled the Spaniards, but their poison stayed behind, and soon we began to die in great numbers. There was wailing and weeping everywhere. The air became rancid with the stench of decaying bodies. Entire families perished. People ran out to the streets or into the lake, hoping to free themselves from the dreadful fire that consumed their bodies. The streets became littered with bodies; the lake became putrid with bloated corpses.

"The pestilence is a painful death. It strikes at the brain, inflaming it, and the body is tortured by fever. The skin is overrun by sores filled with pus. The flesh turns purple, then black, until it splits into runny fissures. Even worse than the pain is the loss of the power to think, and finally, throat and tongue swell until all air is choked out of the victim."

Father Benito's stomach was beginning to hurt because of the woman's vivid descriptions. He remembered that in his childhood, he and his family had been forced to abandon Carmona one summer when the plague broke out. The memory of that experience made his insides twist with pain.

"Señora, I know the signs and effects of the pox. Would you go on to say how the sickness affected the fall of Tenochtitlan?"

"When Moctezuma was assassinated, his brother Cuitlahuac was elected king, but then he became diseased and died. Our people fell into despair because everywhere there was death, and now even the king had been brought down. Cuauhtémoc took the place of king, but by then the once great spirit of the Mexica people had been broken by the white pestilence. The death of its soul is what caused the fall of our city, more than your canons and horses.

"It was then that the gods struck me down as well. I don't know if it was your god or mine, but it was surely a

147

jealous, wrathful god that unleashed punishment on me for my many sins."

As so often happened, the priest was again startled, not only by what Huitzitzilin was saying, but by the intensity of her words. His mind had been concentrating on the fall of the city, but now his thoughts were interrupted by something personal to the woman.

"Please be careful when you invoke God's name, because He is neither jealous nor wrathful. I'll be glad to listen to what you have to say, but I shall not write it because it is personal and no doubt has nothing to do with the history of your people."

Huitzitzilin smiled wryly as she watched the priest put down the quill. She looked at him so long that it made him squirm and rub his face.

"It does have something to do with our history, because I am a Mexica woman. What happened to me happened to most of my people when your people invaded us and cursed us with your sickness."

Father Benito was jarred by the sharpness of the woman's words, and he inwardly scolded himself for again sounding arrogant. But there was nothing he could do about it now. He had offended her, and it could not be undone. He tried to show interest in what she had to say.

"When I returned to my chambers one of those evil days, I found that my son had been stricken by the sickness. What I had feared most happened. He was contaminated even though I had hidden him, even though I had acted like a woman who had no son, in hope of deceiving the grinning menace.

"The pestilence is shrewd; it has the eyes of a tiger, the nose of jackal, the fangs of a coyote, the speed of a snake. It will not be tricked! I saw that the scourge had invaded my own life, and that it had laid its stinking finger on my son's head. On that day his face was bloated and feverish. His tongue struggled to catch air. I gave him water, but he could not drink. I dampened his forehead and cheeks, but I saw that it was of no help. I burned copal, hoping to drive the evil spirit out of my chambers.

"When I saw that my attempts were useless, I implored the gods to take me instead. I begged them to take anything I had, my beauty, my body, my eyes, my spirit, anything except my son. But the child became worse, and I watched him die. What I loved most died. He would not grow to manhood, because he was dead. His intelligence and spirit would not discover the beauty that would surround him, because he was dead, and it was the white beast that had killed him!"

Father Benito reached over and put his hand on Huitzitzilin's shoulder; he realized that she was trembling. He bent down so that he might get a glimpse of her face, but she held it so low that all he could see was her wrinkled forehead.

"You mustn't think of those days. It's too painful."

The woman suddenly straightened up and held her body erect. She lifted her arms menacingly, fists clenched, face pinched. She had jerked forward with so much force that the priest shrank back in his chair.

"Hatred flooded my soul! Like vomit welling in my throat, I felt the desire to run away from Techochtitlan, all the way to the camps of the white men, and there plunge a knife into each one of them.

"Anguish overcame me, and in front of the dead body of my son, I mutilated myself. I tore at my hair until it came out in handfuls. I beat my head against the stone floor. Then I clawed at my face until I punctured one of my eyes. It was with that searing pain that I found some release from the wretchedness caused in me by my son's death."

"Jesus, Mary and Joseph!"

Father Benito made the sign of the cross and was about to get to his feet when Huitzitzilin pushed him back into the chair. He plopped back awkwardly, astonished by her strength.

"I don't know how long I stayed, cursing the gods that had created white men. I only remember that it was the pain in my head that caused me to move. When I got up from the floor, I knew that I could see with only one eye. I also knew that I would now go through life deformed, causing repugnance and pity, and that I would no longer be Huitzitzilin, a woman known for her beauty."

The woman fell into a long silence. Benito slouched in the chair with his eyes closed until he felt Huitzitzilin's hand on his arm. He was struggling with her act of self-mutilation. His mind scurried, looking for a reason, an explanation, but he found none.

When she regained composure, she went on speaking. "Now you can begin writing again because I have a little more to tell about the fall of our city, although it will have to include some of my own story." When the priest frowned she retorted, "I cannot separate what happened to me from the history of my people." Then she waited for him to reach for paper and quill.

"As time passed, the pestilence diminished in vigor, but we had lost the best among the warriors and nobles. Zintle was one of them. We had also lost our spirit, even though we struggled to find our ancient vitality. We made weak attempts at festivity, but our heart was not in it. We pretended to gossip and laugh, but we couldn't deceive one another, because inwardly we grieved for our lost soul.

"Nearly a year passed before Tenochtitlan was again attacked by Captain Cortés, and during that time our people prepared for war. Cuauhtémoc rallied and somehow found the way to initiate new warriors and to accumulate fresh supplies. We stored food, water, clothing and arms in key places of the city.

"As for myself, the wounds on my face healed, but the scars, as you can see for yourself, remained. The socket closed where my eye had been, and in time it became the cavity you now see. I remained part of the court that surrounded the new king, but wagging tongues spoke of my having slept with the white captain. So I felt the coldness around me. It didn't matter to me anyway, because I was filled with grief."

Huitzitzilin appeared to be fatigued. Her body sagged. "I'm going to rest now, but stay for a while because I have more to tell you before you leave."

Father Benito got to his feet and walked to the fountain, where he sat reflecting on what Huitzitzilin had told him. He closed his eyes, but the darkness under his lids was filled with images of war and death, of beauty destroyed and spirits trampled.

Chapter
XVI

Father Benito was surprised when Huitzitzilin called him back to the chair beside her. He had thought that she was too tired, but he saw that a new energy had filled her.

"Strengthened by new allies, Captain Cortés returned during the days when flowers covered Tenochtitlan, but it was to be the last time for our gardens to bloom. The white men came, and our armies were no match because of the plague. Although we were prepared, the long siege reduced us to starvation and thirst, and we could not prevail. Tenochtitlan fell."

"What do you remember about those days?"

"My stomach still shrinks when I remember. It was early morning when the Snake Drum began its warning, telling us that the awaited battle with the invaders was about to begin. The lake filled with war canoes loaded with warriors; the air was charged with their war screams. The causeways were fortified in expectation of the attack, as was every street, house and temple.

"Then the fighting began. Captain Cortés was able to force the Mexica out of the lake with a boat he had constructed and floated. It was loaded with fire-spitting weapons. The battle for the streets of Tenochtitlan, however, was not that easy, and the fighting lasted a long time."

"Nearly three months." Benito spoke softly.

"You know all of the details?"

"Not all. I want to know what happened among your people at that time. What did you eat and when did you sleep? What were you feeling?"

"We were frightened but not afraid. But as the days passed, our losses were so great that the time came when even the wounded went out to fight. We women helped by preparing weapons for the warriors. We also went out to battle, throwing stones and debris at the enemy from rooftops and hidden places. It even happened that we didn't eat or drink so that the men could nourish their bodies with the little food that was left.

"Soon we ran out of food and water. We had nothing to eat except for the bark of trees, plants, and even the weeds from the lake. In time, even these disappeared. Then we had nothing to drink except the water from the lake, but that was salted, so it drove people out of their senses. Then we drank urine.

"Those of us still fighting were pushed back to Tlaltelolco. By that time the canals and streets of the city were destroyed. Our houses, courtyards, meeting places, schools, shrines and temples were no more. And the decaying bodies of our dead reminded us that something much more precious than a city had come to an end. After the captain sent word that we should surrender and save Tenochtitlan, we asked 'What Tenochtitlan?'

"When the end came it was decided that if our city was beyond salvation, an attempt should be made to save the future of our people. A plan was devised for Cuauhtémoc, his wife and others to escape to the northern territories from where we originated. There they would find sanctuary to give birth to a new family. From there the Mexicas in time could reclaim their destiny.

"A canoe was readied. I stood watching as the king, his wife, her women servants and several nobles climbed into it. I stared at them, wondering about my own destiny and what had brought me to that moment to witness the end of my people, as well as the departure of those who would give birth to a new race.

"Then the king asked me to come with them, and I got on the canoe without thinking. No one said anything. It was not a time for complaints or questions, and we all kept silent while the boat made its way toward the northern edge of the lake. But before long, we were caught—trapped, cornered, and captured."

Huitzitzilin stopped speaking, and Father Benito craned his stiff neck. She was again fatigued and unable to go on, but despite this and his own weariness, he wanted to hear more.

"Go on, please! What happened after that?"

"What happened? Cuauhtémoc and the other nobles became prisoners. The rest of us were dispersed in different directions, dying along the way from starvation and sadness. Not long after that, the Mexicas disappeared as a people."

The woman shuddered slightly as she slid her tongue over a dry upper lip. She sighed and got to her feet unsteadily.

"This is all I have to tell you regarding the encounter between my people and yours. From now on you can leave your papers in your monastery, because tomorrow I'll end my confession."

Chapter XVII

"Our gods were vanquished after the fall of Tenochtitlan as were our traditions. Our warriors and nobles were eradicated, our children starved and our women ravished by the white conquerors and their allies. Those of us who survived dispersed, and Anahuac became known as the kingdom of New Spain."

Father Benito sat holding his jaw in one hand. The confessional stole hung limply on his shoulders, almost reaching the ground. He was dismayed by Huitzitzilin's reversal. He had arrived that morning prepared to listen to her confession, only to be hearing more information about *her* history. This time he decided not to say anything, hoping to store what she said in his memory.

"Anahuac became a valley of an evil dream, and we were the dream walkers. It was a world of murder and torture, of defilement and betrayal, of envy and terror. We all participated; no one was free of responsibility. The Mexica hated, and the *Castellanos* lusted. It was during those days that Captain Cortés burned the feet of Cuauhtémoc while trying to force him to reveal the place where a secret treasure was buried. He got nothing out of the king; it is still a secret.

"I was only twenty years of age, but I grew old. I was emaciated, gray strands appeared in my hair and the scars on my face became more pronounced. I was without a home and alone. I tried to return here to this place where I was born, but the roads were clogged and dangerous, so I stayed on the outskirts of what had been the city.

"I did not die, as you can see. Seasons passed during which I was able to make a life. I worked with the crowds of people which the Spaniards put to work rebuilding Tenochtitlan. I was one of the women who carried the stones that had been our temples, palaces and houses from one place to another. In the beginning my hands bled, but then they hardened and I became a good worker. After some years, the city neared its completion and unfortunately work dwindled."

Father Benito's forehead furrowed as he listened. He was picturing the city as he now knew it: the cathedral almost completed, its viceregal palace prominent, its portals crowded with vendors and buyers, as well as a multitude of beggars and thieves. He was envisioning the shrinking lake, now filled with debris, and he tried to imagine how it must have looked when Huitzitzilin was young.

"After that I became a servant. I washed dirty clothes, but it made me sick because I found the stench of the whites intolerable. I was sick almost every day, and because my condition was noticed, I was dismissed. I wandered the streets for weeks, perhaps even months, looking for food and shelter wherever I could. My clothes were rags, and I will admit to you that I begged and ate whatever people cast out of windows and doors. I cursed the white beast and I thought of killing myself."

"Did you ever try to kill yourself?"

"No. Although I repeatedly promised myself that each day would be my last. Sometimes I told myself that I would drown myself in the lake, or that I would cast myself under the the hooves of horses. The answer was always the same. I was a coward and chose to live."

"What did you do then?"

"It happened that one day I was standing in line waiting for food when I saw Baltazar Ovando. He, too, seemed to be expecting something, and I saw that his face had changed. He looked haggard and something in his eyes had changed; no longer sweet, they traveled up and down my body trying to recognize me.

"'Huitzitzilin?' he asked in a whisper."

Father Benito's eyes opened wide, his mouth puckered as he waited for her to continue. But Huitzitzilin hunched back in the chair without saying any more.

"What happened after that?"

"You can't imagine what happed after that?"

The priest flushed, embarrassed at his question. He bit his lip and decided to leave. He stood up.

"Goodbye."

"Goodbye?"

"Yes. I have no reason to be here."

"But there is a reason. You're here to forgive my sins. Please, sit down. I'll begin my confession immediately." The priest patiently obeyed her, sat back in the chair, and straightened the stole. "Before I begin, I must say that at the time I thought he would find me repugnant, but he didn't. So it was that I began my second life with Baltazar Ovando, not as his lover but as something else."

Father Benito nodded in approval, but wondered where the confession would lead. Then his attention was taken by her hands, which were moving, as if drawing a picture.

"He made me one of his servants, but he barely spoke to me. It was only when he needed a woman that he approached me; then we would fornicate."

The woman's offhand declaration of sin had caught the priest by surprise, and he sprang to the edge of the chair so fast that he nearly tipped it over. Making a hasty sign of the cross, he mumbled, "In nomine Patris, et Filii, et Spiritus Sancti."

"Our time together lasted several years. I never really had joy because, although he provided me with shelter, I knew the true reason for that care. Even if my face was disfigured, my body was not. After I regained strength, I became even more beautiful than before the days of starvation—beautiful from the neck down, that is.

"For my part, I can tell you that I never loved Baltazar. But since this is a confession, I will admit that I longed for him. Do you know what I mean?"

Father Benito's face was buried in both hands. A shrug of the shoulders was the only sign he gave Huitzitzilin.

"Since he used my body to relieve his desires, I will be truthful and say that I also satisfied my lust with his body. There was a time during which I lived in expectation of his call, and when it came, I panted with desire."

"Señora, you don't need to give so many details. Your admission of that sin is sufficient. Now, if there are no others, I will absolve..."

"Wait a minute!" Huitzitzilin's voice was edged with irritation. "What makes you think that is all I have to say? You seem to think that a woman and man's coupling is the only sin possible. How absurd!"

Father Benito felt challenged by the woman's haughty manner, and he was on the verge of scolding her, of telling her that fornication is indeed a grievous sin, but he remembered that he was the confessor and she the penitent, and that it was his duty to listen and to forgive. He bit his upper lip and hunched over, his head perched on his left hand.

After a moment, she too relaxed her body and went on speaking. "I conceived. I was not happy when I realized that I was with child by a white man, just like so many of our women who had also had children by the enemy. I hated what was happening to me because I saw that the offspring were disdained by everyone, especially by their fathers. I regretted it also because secretly I thought that such children were ugly.

"I spent a long time remembering my first child and how this second white-brown one would grow in my belly, taking the place of the other one. I cried often and again I hoped to die. When I told Baltazar about the child, he only scowled at me and said that it didn't matter, since it was not the first that he had sired and more than likely not the last.

"It was at that time that Captain Cortés announced that he was leaving Tenochtitlan to head south. The rumor was that his captains had betrayed him and that they were organizing a separate kingdom. The entourage was named; among those accompanying Cortés were Cuauhtémoc, who was nearly an invalid because he never regained the full use of his feet, and Baltazar Ovando.

"I decided that I would also go because I thought that my child should be born in the presence of his father. Baltazar forbade me to come, claiming that it would be too difficult a journey for a woman in my condition. I assured him that I was hardened by work, that I had grown accustomed to not eating, that I was able to tolerate heat and cold and other hardships. Still he refused, but I went anyway."

Father Benito didn't say anything, but he looked at Huitzitzilin quizzically. His expression asked the question.

"Yes, I could go unseen by Baltazar because there were so many people attached to Captain Cortés that it was easy for me to hide among the dozens of servants, secretaries, priests, guards and women that went along as cooks and companions. I'm glad I did it because, unforeseen at the time, I was to witness the death of Cuauhtémoc.

"I've forgotten just how many people were in the captain's train. We were many. First went the captains, armed and mounted on their beasts, then followed the brown-robed priests, then the foot soldiers, their helmets and lances shining in the morning sun. The Tlaxcala allies were part of the group, and after them galloped Captain Cortés, accompanied by his personal guard.

"Behind him walked the women, Spanish as well as our own. Behind us came the personal servants, porters, menders, blacksmiths, cooks, keepers of horses and other animals, scribes, pages, wine-keepers, and two doctors. One couldn't hear what anyone said because of the din created by the clatter of hooves, the baying, bleating and oinking of animals, the shrill laughter of women, the cursing of soldiers, and the crunching of wheels and metal fittings of carts.

"Captain Cortés was by that time acting like a king. On that day he was elegantly attired. His hat was large and round with a long feather that fluttered in the air. His hands were gloved and his shoes were of fine leather. He rode on a large white horse that reared and snorted with anticipation. Everything about him was kingly."

Father Benito was slouched back in his chair, angry at himself for not having brought his writing materials. Although Captain Cortés' trip to Honduras was now part of many chronicles, the priest was aware that the woman was giving special insight. He would try to remember as much as possible, he told himself.

"The entourage marched eastward, crossing mountains, passing the city of Tlaxcala, going through plains, then forging rivers until we reached Coatzocoalcos on the eastern coast. After that, the journey became very difficult because of impassible rivers and even unfriendly villages. Captain Cortés didn't lose courage, however, thinking of what to do every time an obstacle appeared. As you can imagine, many in the group died. People began to grumble, some of them even deserted, especially when the food supplies began to thin out. All of this made Cortés short-tempered and he had men punished severely.

"I was in the early period of my pregnancy and so I was ill often, almost every day. I vomited and felt dizzy, but I was never so sick that I could not continue. I was glad that Baltazar didn't know of my whereabouts. That way I could sleep at night and gather strength.

"We reached the land of the Maya people, a town known as Akalán, which in the language of those people means region of stagnant waters, because several small rivers meet there causing deposits of black, smelly mud. It is an evil place where devils inhabit dead trees. It is a place of lizards and owls, and people who thrive on witchcraft."

Benito's forehead was furrowed and tense because the mere mention of evil caused his body to shudder. He had never before heard of that land, and the woman's descriptions reminded him of paintings depicting hell and purgatory—dark, rank, stinking places.

"We reached a town named Itza Canac, a bleak place deserted many generations before by the Mayas. It was in that foul smelling place that King Cuauhtémoc was murdered by Captain Cortés, who had heeded a rumor that said that the king was hatching a plan to kill him. It was not true, but he and all the white people became terrified, convinced that we would rise again and eat them.

"All of the Mexica, the lords as well as the servants, were summoned by Captain Cortés to the center of camp one night. Without warning, he told us that he had evidence proving that Cuauhtémoc and others of his company were guilty of treason against the king of Spain. At first he spoke normally, but soon his voice sputtered, betraying his terror as he openly accused Cuauhtémoc of treachery. He shouted for a long time until he tired, then he stopped ranting. He turned away from us and took a few steps, then swiveled around and shouted, 'Hang them at dawn!'

"At dawn we gathered in a clearing where there was a muddy stream and a large ceiba tree. When I arrived I caught a glimpse of Cuauhtémoc and another Mexica noble standing under the tree, each with a rope around his neck. At first I thought that Captain Cortés was not there, but I could see that others were there to witness the hanging, among them a certain Bernal Díaz del Castillo, as well as the priest everyone calls Motolinía, and Baltazar Ovando."

Huitzitzilin paused as she put one hand on her chest; she appeared to be out of breath. Father Benito took the moment to reflect on what she had just said about a priest, and he felt his curiosity aroused because he had never heard that name before.

"Señora, what was the priest's name?"

"Motolinía."

"What was his family name?"

"I don't know. We all knew him only by that name."

"But it's not a Christian surname. Surely, he must have had a proper name had he been Spanish."

"Perhaps. Nonetheless, I remember him only as Father Motolinía." Huitzitzilin shifted in the chair and returned to her story.

"Those of us who were Mexica were quiet, as if under a spell. It was Cuauhtémoc's voice that brought us to our senses. He said something like, 'Cortés, you meant to do this from the beginning.' I stretched my neck because I thought that the captain was not there, but then I saw him standing with the other captains.

"He said nothing. Instead he motioned to the soldiers holding the rope. I saw both bodies suddenly leap into the air. Their arms were bound to their bodies, but their legs were loose and they jerked violently. Gurgling sounds escaped from their throats, and their bodies convulsed, trying to keep the life that was ebbing out of them. Soon the struggle ended and the bodies hung limp, lifeless.

"I recall that I felt numb as I bent my head back to look up at the struggling body of the last king of the Mexicas. When I saw his purple, quivering face, its tongue hanging out of his mouth like the liver of a beast, I remembered my own mutilation and I thought of how we had once been a beautiful people, but were now deformed.

"I looked around and saw that those who remained were all weeping. With their hands covering their faces, they cried, and some had fallen on their knees and elbows. Then I saw Father Motolinía. He, too, was crying, but soon he controlled himself and instructed us to take down the bodies. Without a word, we placed them on litters and, despite the probability of punishment, we began our journey northward to Cuauhtémoc's place of birth, which is here, where you and I are seated."

Father Benito looked around, expecting to see the ghosts of that long-ago funeral cortege wind its way into the convent garden. He shook his head in amazement at what Huitzitzilin was telling him. Now he knew that he would not forget any part of the story, even though he was not writing it.

"We retraced our steps, stopping only to rest and eat. One of those places was Cumuapa, where Maya physicians assisted us with their knowledge of preparing the bodies so that corruption would not set in. The process was long and intricate, taking several days, but we waited without complaints. After the medications had been applied, the doctors wrapped the bodies in cotton material, then encased them in boxes made of aromatic wood. It was only then that we renewed our journey.

"After a few months, the time had come for me to have my baby, and the entourage waited for me. To my surprise, there came not one child but two: a boy and a girl. But this time there was no joy. I didn't even name them; they remained nameless for for several years. I just called them Little Boy and Little Girl.

"In the beginning, Father Motolinía insisted that the children be baptized, but I refused. He waited patiently and in the end he prevailed, christening not only them but me as well. The boy received the name Baltazar, the girl Paloma, and I was named María de

Belén. I never called them by those names, and persisted in calling them little this or little that.

"In the beginning, I didn't feel love for those children, because they appeared strange to me. Their heads seemed different, oddly shaped, as were their eyes. Their bones seemed too long. When their teeth began to show, I saw that those, too, were shaped and colored in a way that I didn't like. The color of their skin was faded, the girl's especially, and as they grew, these deformities became more prominent.

"I saw that my people laughed at my children when they thought that I was not looking or listening, and I was angry. I felt that way not because of the mockery, which I understood, seeing that the children were indeed ugly, but because of having lusted after Baltazar Ovando. The boy and girl were the result of my weakness.

"It took us years to arrive here, and to this day I don't know how we did it. We were attacked by thieves and even chased by hostile villagers who thought that we were diseased outcasts because we were so ragged and emaciated. We lost our way several times, and many in our group died of starvation or fatigue.

"When we arrived here, the children were four-years old and I looked ten years older than I really was. We had all thought that we would be happy once in Coyoacán, but we weren't, because what we found was a blighted place, a village ruined by the white soldiers. No one was around. Everyone had been killed or had fled to the mountains, and there was no one to pay homage to the remains of the king whom we had returned to his place of birth. There was nothing but waste, hunger, and dead memories.

"It's my understanding that Father Motolinía wrote an account of our wanderings and of the final place of Cuauhtémoc's remains. I've heard said that he entrusted that chronicle to the people of Coyoacán. Perhaps you'll find it of interest.

"As for myself and my children, I walked them through the village of my birth, showing them what remained of the palace of my family. It was in ruins, so we left. I did not return to it until my old age. And you can see for yourself, a convent has now been built over those ruins."

"The woman spoke of Father Motolinía, who apparently witnessed the events leading to the execution of King Cuauhtémoc. She claims that the priest wrote an account and turned it over to the people of Coyoacán."

Father Benito was speaking to Father Anselmo as they strolled through the olive grove attached to the monastery. It was early evening, and both men had their arms tucked deep into the sleeves of their habit because of the growing chill in the air. Anselmo had the cowl pulled over his bald head. Vespers were soon to begin. Even so, Benito took his time speaking because he was anxious to ask the older priest about Motolinía.

"Father Anselmo, I've never heard of such a priest, have you?"

The older monk was silent for several minutes. Only the crunch of dried leaves mashing against pebbles filled the air. "Yes, I've heard of him. He was among the first of our brothers to come to this land. He did much for the natives of the mission. He wrote accounts of their ways. Most of his books are in Seville, along with other important histories written on the subject of the discovery and conquest of this continent. I believe he died nearly twenty years ago."

Benito lowered his head to peer under the overhanging hood shrouding Father Anselmo's features. "I thought that I had read most of the chronicles while still in Seville. I don't understand why my teachers never spoke of Father Motolinía nor of his writings."

"That's because Motolinía was not our brother's real name. It was Father Toribio de Benavente."

Benito stopped abruptly, almost tripping as one of his sandals caught under a heap of pebbles. He took hold of Anselmo's elbow, making him stop also.

"Father Toribio de Benavente! Of course I know his name, and his work as well." He paused, licked his upper lip and blinked several times. "Where on earth did the name Motolinía come from?"

"The natives gave him that name. The word means "the poor one" in their tongue. You see, Benavente grew to love these people so much that he lived like them, ate like them, learned their language and became poor like them. They in turn took him in, as if he had been one of their own."

Father Benito felt moved. He had wanted to do the same thing from the beginning, from the moment he first listened to God's call for him to become a monk. He had secretly vowed to dedicate his life to the people of this land when he had been assigned to come here. He had promised to become one of them.

Benito interrupted his reflections to discuss the Benavente chronicle. That document, Huitzitzilin said, was based on the events surrounding the death and burial of the last Mexica king. If so, Benito told himself, the value of the book would be significant.

"As I've said, the woman spoke of an account written by Father Benavente, one entrusted to the people of Coyoacán. Such a work is surely of great value and should be sent to Seville, don't you agree?"

"Certainly! But what makes you so sure of its existence?"

"Why..."

"Because a distracted old woman has said it exists?"

"I would think..."

"Father Benito, try to think clearly! Firstly, the woman told you that the chronicle was entrusted to the people of Coyoacán. We *are* in Coyoacán. If such a work existed, it would be in the holdings of one place only, our monastery. Secondly, if he did write such an account, I cannot believe that Father Benavente would have so foolishly left his work in the hands of uninformed natives. Even if he did think of them as his children, he was an erudite man; he knew the historical value of his work."

Anselmo stopped speaking to reflect a little more. Then he looked at Benito, eyebrows arched. "I'm convinced that the woman is wrong, that such a history was never written, and that Seville has all of Benavente's works. All of them!"

The bell calling the monks to vespers began tolling, and the two monks turned toward the monastery chapel. The ringing also marked the commencement of the Grand Silence, so both men walked side by side without uttering a word. When they entered the chapel, it was

173

filled with candlelight. The stone pillars cast elongated shadows on the golden tiers of the altar and on the tabernacle surrounded by round-faced cherubs.

Father Benito went to his assigned pew, took the Office Book in his hands, made the sign of the cross and responded to the soft *Ave María* sung out by the lead chanter. Along with the other monks, he mouthed the prayers that followed, but he was thinking of Huitzitzilin, of Cuauhtémoc, of Motolinía and of a possibly missing chronicle.

Chapter XIX

Father Benito arrived at the convent earlier than usual the next morning. He had rushed through his prayers and other duties at the monastery, anxious to get to Huitzitzilin and her continuing story. When he stepped into the garden, he saw that she was strolling through the shadowy archways of the cloister. She seemed to be conversing with someone.

He stood gazing at her for a while, smiling because he was certain that she was speaking with her spirits. He didn't believe in that part of the old woman's story, but he told himself that if she needed company, what could be better than the invention of phantoms that returned to her from the past. Then, on the spur of the moment, he decided to move closer to hear what she was saying. He moved slowly, careful not to step on a stone or leaf that would signal his approach.

When he was close enough to hear Huitzitzilin, he discovered that she was not only speaking but singing as well. Her words were in her native tongue and Benito could not understand. He could tell, however, that there was joy in her words. As she moved, she gestured with her hands and nodded in agreement. Sometimes she paused, as if listening, then she responded.

After a while Benito felt embarrassed: he had been spying on her. He decided to return to his chair and wait there for her. He was grateful that he had brought paper and quill that day, and he intentionally made noises as he unpacked his leather bag.

Huitzitzilin's attention was caught by the sound of rustling paper as well as the scraping of Benito's chair, and she snapped out of her reverie. She looked at him from across the garden, a smile curving her thin lips. She walked over to the priest, greeted him, and took her place beside him.

"I was speaking with them."

"With whom, Señora?"

"With the spirits of my children."

Father Benito stared at the woman, concluding that the twins had also died. He furrowed his forehead in sympathy.

"I'm sorry."

"Why? They're still here. Look over there. They think you look foolish."

Benito's head snapped in the direction in which Huitzitzilin was pointing, but he saw only the crystalline drops of water splashing over the sides of the fountain. But he could not help feeling the sting her words had caused him.

"Foolish? Why do they think that?" His eyebrows arched haughtily, betraying his offended feelings.

"I don't know. The spirits are difficult to discern."

Song of the Hummingbird

Huitzitzilin's response only served to annoy Benito more, but he decided to move on to the closure of her story. He placed a stack of paper on his lap, dipped the quill in the ink pot and, without saying anything, prepared to set down whatever she had to say. He had decided during the previous night that he would record everything in his chronicle. And now, since he felt offended, he told himself that he would write down even her sins.

"Four years passed before Paloma, Baltazar and I returned to Tenochtitlan. On that day, I held them by the hand as we walked into what had once been the most beautiful city of our world. My children, who had never seen such a place, stared with eyes as large as suns and asked, 'How can that be so big? Who built this? Why are there so many people here?'

"Everything was big, but not beautiful. Tenochtitlan was now a clutter of unsightly buildings, churches, and convents, all of which had massive doors and gates; all the windows had bars on them, as if in constant expectation of thieves or intruders. The streets were no longer straight, but curved in baffling mazes that often led nowhere. Our temples, shrines, and palaces were either modified beyond recognition or demolished, their stones used for residences and monasteries. The stink of the lake was overwhelming, unbearable, its waters blackened with squalid refuse and with animal as well as human excrement. Gone were the canoes filled with flowers and vegetables, gone the merchants, vendors, and fishermen.

"The streets of the city were congested. We were jostled and pressed against walls by rude people. There were carts and wagons as well as elegant coaches for ladies and gentlemen. The children wondered out loud when they saw not only horses, but other varieties of that beast: burros and mules. The air was filled with shouting, creaking, banging, and the new language could be heard everywhere. I was beginning to learn it myself and, although I didn't speak it as I do now, I could tell that what people screamed at one another was offensive and dirty. I discovered at that time that the city had been renamed Mexico. I was grateful for that much; at least the name of my people would not be forgotten along with everything else that was ours.

"During the years of our wandering, I had to find food and shelter on the road for us, and that had not been easy. I again worked as a servant for your people, who by then were arriving in this land in multitudes. When I worked at that, I found out that Spanish women are demanding, that they appreciate their finery, but that they dislike washing their own clothes or cleaning what they dirty.

"During those years I came to understand many things, one being that most of the men and women that came here from your country were poor in their land. When I made that discovery, I found it strange, because here they act disdainful and domineering.

"After we buried Cuauhtémoc, the children and I went away and stayed mostly in Michoacán, the land of lakes. We didn't find the hardships there that we had encountered elsewhere because the people of that region are kind, less angry. I think it's because there is more food and space in which to live. Because of this I decided to stay there and work, mostly in fish markets. I did several things, but mostly I fished and cooked my catch, making a life for my children and for myself that way.

"I don't know why I left that place. I can only say that my heart yearned for Tenochtitlan. I was, I am, a Mexica, and we can never be for long separated from our world. So I saved what money I could, and when I thought that I had what was sufficient, I made my way north.

"Also, I must admit that I returned in search of the children's father. I thought that he would want to see them, and in my foolish imagination I even hoped that he would want me to be by his side. At that time I still did not understand how much your people disdain us, those of us who are native to these lands. I as yet was mindless enough to think that Baltazar would consider me as a wife."

Father Benito stopped writing and looked at Huitzitzilin. "Why would you want to be by his side? It's clear that neither of you had ever cared for one another."

"I don't know. I was alone and saw how many women like me had married Spaniards, and they lived a regular life. But you're right, I had never loved Baltazar. At that time I convinced myself that if I had tolerated being with Tetla, why not Baltazar."

"Did you find him?"

"Yes. It wasn't difficult to find him because by that time he had received large parcels of land and he was wealthy and well-known. I was told that his hacienda was located in Xochimilco. I also found out something else. Baltazar had sent to Spain for a wife, a girl who had been his love since childhood. She was known among my people for her fine taste, her beautiful dresses, her gilded coach and horses, her piety and, of course, her arrogance. I also was told that even though she and Baltazar had been married for several years, they were childless. It was said that she was dry."

"Dry?"

"Yes. But I see, young priest, that you don't know what I mean. I think that it is best if I don't explain it."

Father Benito decided not to pursue his question when he understood that she was talking about something that happened only to women. He told himself that it was better for him not to dwell on such matters; instead he concentrated on writing what he was hearing.

"I will not deny it: I felt jealous. I don't know why, because as I have already told you, I did not love Baltazar as I had Zintle. Still, there was something; it could have been the memories or even the pleasure that he had given me. Also, there were the children who were his, and I told myself that he should know them, especially since he did not have other babies.

"There was one thing that I feared, however, and that was the possibility of Baltazar denouncing me to Captain Cortés for having abandoned the expedition in the south. He could have done that, since we were as yet considered guilty of desertion, and the punishment for that was having one's feet cut off. I thought of this carefully, but I put my fear aside and decided to approach him with the intention of letting him know of our existence.

"Baltazar's home was beautiful. It was surrounded by gardens filled with flowers. The path leading to the entrance was shaded by trees, and inside the gate there were several fountains that were interconnected by canals of running water. I remember that there were birds of all colors and sizes in cages everywhere. The house was different from what we used to have in that it had bars on all the windows, but the corridors that surrounded its walls were filled with flowers and greenery, just like ours used to be.

"Once there, I became afraid to make myself known. My courage failed me. I think that I had been a servant for too long a time by then, and the Spanish masters intimidated me. So with the children I went to the rear of the house, hoping to find the kitchen. I discovered that it was not attached to the house but stood by itself. Later on I was told that the mistress of the house hated the smell of food, and she insisted that all the cooking be done outside.

"When I found one of the servants, I asked for Don Baltazar Ovando, but I was not immediately attended because everyone was rushing here and there with different tasks that had to be done. There were countless servants and even slaves: not only Mexica, but Otomí, Chichimeca, Huasteca, and even some of the northern people known as Yaqui. There were also the black ones that had been brought over in the floating houses."

Benito put down the quill and took a deep breath. "Señora, forgive my interruption, but will these details lead to something important?"

"You find what I'm telling you unimportant?"

"Not exactly. I'm sure that to you everything that has happened in your life is important, but..."

"But what? Is what happened to me and to others like me not interesting to you?"

"Please! Don't be offended! It's not a matter of what is interesting or uninteresting, but rather what is historical. I'm here to gather as much material as I can to write a chronicle of the same magnitude as those written by Fathers Sahagún and De las Casas."

"Who are they?"

"Priests who have written of what happened in this land when our captains arrived."

"How do they know what happened? Were they present as I was when things took place?"

"In some cases yes, and in others no."

"And you consider that historical?"

Father Benito was about to retort something, but decided against it because he knew that he was on the verge of losing his temper. Instead, he clamped his mouth shut, hearing the dull clank of his own teeth. He breathed deeply again and prepared to listen to Huitzitzilin instead of writing. He told himself that if he judged something of historical value, he would put it on paper. He turned to her and nodded.

Huitzitzilin smiled smugly knowing that she had won the skirmish, and began where she had left off. "Breaking into the flurry of activity, I again asked for the master. This time someone went to tell him that someone was asking for him in the kitchen. Baltazar did not come to where I was, but sent word for me to be shown into a small room that was located at the far side of the house.

"I walked in and I saw that he too had aged. His hair was no longer light and plentiful; instead it was gray, and there were spots that were bald. He had grown heavy, and his face had filled out. His beard accentuated this because it had thickened, and he wore it longer than before.

"When he realized who it was that he was facing, his eyes filled with disdain and repugnance, but it didn't matter to me because I knew that my feelings towards him were also bad. I found him vulgar. Cruelty was stamped on his face, and his mouth was tight, showing deep lines. Above all, his eyes were fierce, angry, and extremely annoyed. How much did I regret having found him!"

Father Benito's irritation had subsided, and he began to take interest in what Huitzitzilin was saying. Her description of the Spanish captain was so vivid that he was visualizing Ovando, and he agreed that the man was indeed vulgar and cruel.

"How many years had passed since you last saw Ovando?"

"More than five, and much had happened to us both. We looked older than we were." She paused and looked at him. Benito saw that her good eye was brighter than usual. "Do you want to hear more?"

The monk realized that Huitzitzilin was being play-
ful and went along with her humor. "Yes. Please go on."

"Baltazar neither greeted me nor asked for my wel-
fare. It was as if he had seen me only that morning.
With a cold glance he looked at me from my head to my
feet and then up again. Only when he turned to the children did his eyes betray something. What I saw in that
look was curiosity, especially since they were obviously a
mixture of brown and white. But he didn't acknowledge
them or say a word. When he had finished staring at us,
he walked to the door and began to open it, but stopped
short. He turned to look at me.

"'Are they baptized?'

"When I assented with a nod, he asked, 'What are
their names?'

"You won't believe me, but for a moment I could not
remember what Father Motolinía had named them, but
soon I responded, 'Baltazar and Paloma.' Then he
walked out of the room, slamming the door behind him.

"After that I hardly saw him. I did receive word that
I could stay on the premises, that I and the children
were to be given shelter, clothing, and food in exchange
for which I was to work in the laundry. Even though I
felt the sting of humiliation, I stayed there because my
children and I had nowhere else to go.

"It was a time of hardship, not only for me but for
all who were servants in that household. We were forced
to do work that was so difficult that our bodies ached
almost always. Our day began at dawn when we were
called by the bells to attend Mass. Although no one
wanted to do this, we had no choice. So we shuffled into

the chapel and waited. When the master and his wife appeared through a side door, the priest would begin his mutterings."

"Señora, you mean prayers. A priest does not mutter; he prays."

"Whatever you say. All I know is that we were obliged to learn, by heart, the responses to what he said."

"That is common practice throughout this land, and it's good because now you are all united in one spirit, one church. You know that through those prayers God will understand you."

"Well, priest, only God could understand, because we didn't. None of us knew what we were mumbling, but we parroted the words, because if we did not do so, a spy would tell on us, and that meant a lash with a whip, or even being deprived of food for the day. So we mouthed words that we didn't understand while we suppressed yawns.

"When Baltazar's wife walked into the chapel, our sleep-filled eyes opened in wonder because she was always surrounded by pages and a multitude of maids. She was not beautiful to us, but now I understand that in the eyes of a Spaniard she was considered extremely lovely. We, of course, saw her differently. Her skin was colorless, like polished white stone. She was very thin, and too tall to be a woman. Her nose was short and her mouth was too small; its lips were the color of a monkey's liver. Her eyes were blue and too round, like those of a large tapir. Her hair was the color of gold, and we were all certain that it was as stiff and cold as that metal.

"Despite her desire to appear pious, we all knew that it was only an appearance because she was not kind. She disliked us very much, especially our children, whom she pinched and hit. She often hit them on the head with closed fists, and she even kicked them. This happened several times to Baltazar and Paloma.

"Days turned into months without any change in my life until the time when I was sent word by the master to come to his study. He was seated at his writing table scribbling on a paper. He didn't say anything as I stood gazing at him.

"When he finished writing, he said, 'My wife and I have no children.' Then he stared at me for a long time. I didn't answer because something inside of me warned me of danger. He went on to say more. 'It's my intention to take Baltazar and Paloma as my own. They're my blood and are entitled to be my inheritors.' Those words have been scorched into my heart since then."

Benito was mute, even though he rebuked himself for not saying something that might express understanding. The truth was that he knew of many similar cases. Seville was constantly receiving Spanish offspring of native women, especially boy children.

"That is exactly what Baltazar told me. He also said that the paper that he had in front of him was the order to secure passage for the children back to Spain, where he would make certain that their minds and spirits became Christian."

Huitzitzilin's voice faded until it became a whisper. Benito was observing her and he noticed that she was not as agitated as he would have expected. Instead he saw that she was calm, even resigned. When she spoke up, her voice had regained its normal tone.

"I have told you that I considered the children repugnant, but that was only in the beginning. By the time their father wanted them, I had grown to love them. I had carried them in my belly. I had nourished and cared for them. They were my flesh and spirit, and they were the only things I had in this world.

"Then I did something that I have regretted all my life. I humiliated myself in front of him. I fell on my knees and implored him not to do it. The children were frail, I told him; they would die without me. I tried to appeal to his heart, to whatever sentiment he had ever felt for me, and I begged. It was to no avail, because he remained unmoved and instead told me to get out.

"The next day two men and a woman of your race came in a coach and took the children. As you can imagine, they wept and clung to me, but I could do nothing, and they were taken from me. They were put into the coach, but I could see them struggling to get out. They were crying, and their mouths were distorted with fear. The last recollection I have is of their faces looking back at me. "

"Did you ever see them again?"

"Years later I saw Paloma. I'll tell you about that tomorrow, because I feel fatigued this afternoon. Will you return?"

"Yes."

Father Benito stood and helped Huitzitzilin to her feet. As he took her elbow and walked a short span of the cloister with her, thoughts of children who were sent to Spain crowded into his mind. He looked at the woman beside him and he wondered why, in the countless lessons and instructions given to him about this land, no one had explained that its natives loved and grieved as did his people.

Chapter
XX

"What I have to say to you today will perturb you."

"Señora, a priest's duty is to listen, not judge."

Huitzitzilin looked steadily at Father Benito. Her eye narrowed to a slit—she seemed to be debating inwardly. After a while she nodded in agreement and began to speak.

"I laid on my sleeping mat for days after the children were taken away. I neither slept nor ate nor drank nor moved. I prayed that I would die. I was filled with hatred, and I vowed that I would do something to make Baltazar pay for what he had done. I swore that he would feel a greater pain than the one that was tormenting me."

Father Benito took out the stole that was tucked into the leather pouch and draped the cloth around his shoulders. The passion with which Huitzitzilin was expressing herself gave him reason to listen as confessor and not as scribe.

"But what could I do to punish Baltazar for the grief that he had committed against me? I hated them both: the man and the woman. I despised her dryness and I detested his cruelty. Then I began offerings to Mictlanci-huatl."

Father Benito's eyes widened and his jaw set, giving him a stern expression. Now he was certain that this was indeed a matter for confession, and he was relieved that he had foreseen it.

"Who or what is Mic...Mic..."

He could not pronounce the word. But he sensed that it was something connected with the religious beliefs that were held before the gospel of redemption reached Huitzitzilin's people. It was against this that Father Anselmo had cautioned. Once more, the woman had caught Benito unprepared.

"Mictlancihuatl is the goddess of Hell."

"Señora!"

"Yes! I repeat that I prayed and made offerings to her, imploring her to come to my assistance, to fill me with the evil of a multitude of demons. I begged her to enlighten me as to how to deal the blow that would avenge my sufferings."

"You were a Christian by then, and you knew that your thoughts were sinful. You were aware, I'm certain, that wishing evil on another is a mortal sin. Our Lord Jesus said..."

"Sin or no sin, it mattered little to me!"

Huitzitzilin cut off Benito's words, and she kept quiet for a while as if expecting him to go on, but he didn't. He appeared to be angry and unwilling to say more.

"Then I slipped into a stupor that lasted for days until something happened that cast me further down into Hell."

"Jesus, Mary and Joseph!"

Huitzitzilin, oblivious to Father Benito's words, went on speaking. "A voice came to me, telling me to rise from my mat, that something terrible had occurred, that my son Baltazar had died. The coach that carried him and his sister crashed into a ravine and the boy perished. The voice told me that only Paloma had survived the accident.

"Hearing of my son's death jolted me out of that black dream, and, strangely, I knew what I was to do. Mictlancihuatl had come to my assistance. My vision became as sharp as that of the eagle or of the tiger that sees its prey and prepares to devour it. I rose from the mat filled with the desire to inflict not only the pain which Baltazar had caused me, but a suffering magnified countless times. I knew what to do."

"To be filled with evil is to be possessed by Satan, and to hate is a capital sin. Did you not understand that the passion to which you yielded put your soul in jeopardy? You should have sought the counsel of a priest."

"No! A priest would have sided with Baltazar, just as you are now doing. He would have told me to resign myself and to offer my pain in atonement for my sins. A priest is a man, a Spanish man, and he would have told on me."

"You're wrong! I am not siding with him. And besides, don't you understand that what is said in confession is sealed forever? A priest, when hearing a confession, takes the place of God, and he never betrays the confidence of a sinner."

"I didn't believe it then, nor do I believe it now!"

Father Benito stared at Huitzitzilin. He was dumbfounded. He wanted to reprimand her, but she had spoken with such intensity that he couldn't find a response. He felt useless, ridiculous. He was hearing the confession of a sinner who did not believe in his power to forgive. An uneven sigh wheezed through his nose.

"I listened to the voice of Mictlancihuatl, who instructed me. I called one of my fellow servants and asked for help, and he agreed. I told him to brag that he knew where the treasure of Cuauhtémoc was hidden. If he did this enough times, the gossips would see to it that it reached Baltazar's hearing.

"The man did as I told him, and as I had predicted, word reached Baltazar and he called the man to his presence. He questioned him closely, repeatedly, in the beginning with skepticism and then, gradually, with belief. He was greedy, and just as Mictlancihuatl had foreseen, it proved to be his demise, because he fell into my trap.

"Baltazar ordered the servant to take him to the treasure. Did Ovando take the precaution of having at least one other person with him to provide assistance in the case of danger? No! That would have placed him in the position of having to share the treasure. Instead he followed alone, convinced that he had discovered what even Captain Cortés could not find.

"Following my instructions, the servant led Baltazar to Tlaltelolco, the place where Cuauhtémoc had made his last battle and which was still in ruins. In fact, to this day there are hidden corridors and buried vaults known only to our people. It was to that place that Baltazar followed the servant.

"He was led to the entrance of a collapsed palace, through several rooms, then on to a hallway, down through an opening to stairs that descended into a chamber in the bowels of the earth. There the servant told Baltazar to wait while he went ahead to open the last entry leading to the treasure. Shortly after the man left, Ovando heard the bang of a closing door. And there he waited...and waited...and waited."

As Father Benito listened, he felt his body tensing because he sensed what had happened to Baltazar. He didn't interrupt Huitzitzilin because he was afraid that she might change her mind and not confess the whole story.

"The chamber door through which the servant had exited was firmly sealed behind him, but it had a small panel. It was through that opening that I was able to see, to hear, to smell, to savor the agony of Baltazar Ovando. When he realized what was happening, he began to shout and pound on the door with his fists. Time passed, and I listened as fear gripped his heart. It wasn't until hours later that I let him know that I was on the other side of the door.

"I said to him through the opening, 'Baltazar, it is I, Huitzitzilin. This is my gift to you in return for having stolen my children.' That's all I said before he scrambled to the door, beating and kicking at it while he ordered me to free him. His arrogance did not last long; soon he pleaded and begged me to release him. I didn't respond. My silence was the answer to his sniveling. I closed the panel and walked away from that tomb."

"You left him there?"

"Yes."

"He died?"

"Yes."

Father Benito closed his eyes, trying to grasp the fact that the old woman seated in front of him had committed murder. His mind darted in different directions, hoping to discover words to say, but it was no use, because all he could comprehend was that a captain of Spain had been snared into a slow, excruciating death, and that the assassin had been Huitzitzilin.

"Why did the captain not take someone with him? His death might have been avoided had he been accompanied."

"I've already told you. He was greedy and would not take the chance of having to share the treasure with anyone."

"Why did that servant—your accomplice—obey you, knowing that it was murder? Did he not fear being chastised and even put to death?"

"Baltazar was hated by all of his servants. It was easy to find someone to help do away with him, even at the risk of punishment."

"Why did the captain believe the servant so readily? Did he not understand that the treasure might not exist?"

"His greed blinded him just as it still happens with most of your captains."

Father Benito ran out of questions. He was perplexed. He thought for a long while of what to say. His knowledge of the law was limited, but he knew that the woman's deed was even now liable to severe punishment. He reminded himself then, that he was a priest, a confessor, and not a judge or an executioner. His voice faded to a whisper.

"Murder is not only a mortal sin but a capital offense. You know what happens to murderers in Spain, don't you?"

"Are you going to betray me?"

Benito's eyes narrowed as he stared at Huitzitzilin. Again, his mind groped. She had committed murder, and the thought of it appalled him, despite the fact that she had been provoked by the captain.

"What would we do if all the mothers deprived of their children murdered the men responsible?"

Benito had not meant to blurt out what he was thinking, but the words slipped through his lips. He saw that Huitzitzilin was momentarily confused. She was waiting for an answer, not a question. She repeated her query.

"Are you going to betray me?"

"No. My lips are sealed by the sacrament of penance."

"Will you forgive me?"

"God forgives all sins if there is contrition."

"But will *you* forgive me?"

Huitzitzilin's persistence unnerved Benito, and he tried to evade her question. He understood that he didn't have an answer because he was horrified by her revelation in spite of his obligation to forgive her in the name of God. Yet, it was not God's pardon that she was demanding; it was his, and he couldn't find that forgiveness, no matter how much he looked into his soul.

"Señora, I'm not feeling well. I'll return tomorrow to finish your confession."

As he stood, Benito felt his knees shaking and his head aching. He walked away from Huitzitzilin carefully, taking one step at a time. He feared he would trip and fall.

Chapter
XXI

"Brother, I can see that you are in greater anguish than ever. Is it the Indian woman?"

Father Benito's eyes squinted as he gazed at Anselmo, mostly because the older monk's discernment amazed him and partly because of the declining rays of the sun. Anselmo had come upon Benito a few meters from the entrance to the monastery, where Benito had been walking with head hung low. When the porter opened the gate, the two monks walked towards the inner cloister. Father Anselmo invited Benito into his cell. Once inside, Anselmo pointed to a small bench.

"Please take a seat."

Anselmo remained standing with his hands clasped, finger tips pressed together. It was the posture he took whenever he was addressing the monks in his position as prior.

"Do you want to talk about it?"

"Forgive me, Father, but it concerns the woman's confession."

"I see."

Anselmo's body softened as he turned to gaze out the window cut into the stone wall of the cell. There was a long silence before he spoke again.

"Brother, the seal of confession is a heavy burden, one that only the Spirit can alleviate. Put yourself in God's hands, and He will deliver you from the weight that I sense bearing down on you."

Huitzitzilin's words describing the murder of Captain Ovando echoed in Benito's mind despite telling himself over and again that the awful deed had been committed so many years before that it should be forgotten as well as forgiven. He nonetheless struggled with the issue of justice. Should she not have been punished for what she did?

"Father, have you ever heard a confessed sin so grievous that you have found it beyond your forgiveness?"

Anselmo reflected on the question for a while before answering. "It is not for us to forgive. That is for God alone to do."

"Yet, how can we, mere flesh and blood, presume God's forgiveness if we, in our hearts, cannot find that same pardon? What I mean to say is that if I raise my hand in absolution knowing that my heart detests the evil committed by the sinner, how can I tell if God is forgiving that person?"

"We know that God forgives precisely for the reason you've just given. Our Father hates the sin, not the sinner who is victimized by evil. When this distinction is made, mercy follows easily."

Father Anselmo pursed his lips, confident that he had responded appropriately to Benito's question. When he began to move from where he stood, however, the younger priest spoke up with another barrage of questions.

"But are we priests not God's instruments? And if we are, then is it not true that we should feel God's pardon coursing through our soul and mind? And if this does not happen, is it not true that we should conclude that God has remained unforgiving?"

"Father Benito, one moment, please! One question at a time."

Anselmo raised his hand in midair, its white, tapered fingers casting a luminous aura against the dark wall of the cell. He moved to a chair and sat next to Benito, the better to look into his eyes. He then realized that most of the daylight had diminished. He stretched his arm until he reached a candle on his writing table, struck a flint and lit the wick. When he leaned back, he again put his hands together at the finger tips.

"We must conclude one thing only when hearing a penitent's confession, and that is to absolve. When there is contrition, then we know that God will most certainly forgive."

"And if there is no contrition?"

Anselmo arched his thin eyebrows in astonishment. "Why would anyone confess a sin if there is no contrition? That would be a contradiction."

Silence filled the stony cell while Benito searched his thoughts, wondering about Huitzitzilin's motives for having confessed the sin of murder. He was unsure that

it had been remorse or sorrow. Then he looked at Anselmo as if wanting to speak, but the older priest held up
his hand in a gesture that silenced him. Fearing that
Benito was dangerously close to divulging the secrets
that should remain buried in his soul, Anselmo decided
to end the conversation.

"Brother, continue your transcription of the Indian
woman's chronicle. Leave the forgiveness of her sins to
our most merciful Lord, who loves all His children in
equal measure."

Father Benito got to his feet, nodded in agreement,
and walked to the door. "Good night, Reverend Father,
and thank you. I'll reflect on what you have said."

"Good night, Brother."

Benito spent the night sleeplessly as he wrestled
with the idea that Huitzitzilin should have been put to
justice. As the night passed, his thoughts relived the
days he had spent with the Indian woman. The events of
her life, as well as the people she had described, glided
from one side of his cell to the other. Tetla, Cuauhtémoc,
Zintle, Cortés, Ovando, her sons, her daughter, all of the
people Huitzitzilin had evoked in his imagination
marched in front of the priest's eyes.

He tried to sleep, but it was useless. After hours of
trying to doze, he abandoned the struggle, lit a candle,
and went to the table where he had stacked the pages
that held the woman's story. He scanned the manuscript
at random, beginning with the Hill of the Star, review-
ing her words on the ways and beliefs of her people,
their homes and temples, her marriage, loves and grief.

With each line, Benito felt more captivated by Huitzitzilin's words.

He was staring at the last page when the bell for matins began to ring; it was dawn. Huitzitzilin's story, he realized, was unfinished and he knew that it was for him to record that ending. When he stood up from the table, his legs were cramped by the damp chill of the cell. They ached, but he paid little attention to his discomfort because he was thinking of the woman's story and her insistence on his forgiveness.

"Have mercy on us, O Lord, and in your bounty forgive our transgressions."

Father Anselmo's prayer began the early morning chant, and as Benito took his place in the choir, he felt the power of Huitzitzilin's life permeate him. Making the sign of the cross and bowing in expectation of the prior's blessing, the young monk put aside his preoccupation with justice and concentrated on the gift of mercy.

Chapter
XXII

"Good morning, Señora."

Huitzitzilin looked at Benito; her gaze was cheerful. She smiled at him.

"Good morning, young priest. I see that you've changed."

"Changed? What do you mean?"

"You've grown wiser."

As always, the woman's forthright response caused Benito embarrassment. But this time he decided to pursue rather than dodge her remark.

"How can a person grow wiser overnight?"

"By accepting what is in here." She pointed to her chest with her index finger. When Benito gawked at her, she continued speaking. "Have you forgiven me?"

His face flushed until the high ridges of his ears turned a purplish hue, and he shook his head expressing his emotions. Benito felt a mix of admiration and uneasiness at the way the woman could read what was stirring inside of him. He had to clear his throat before speaking, but his voice was thin.

"Yes, I have forgiven you. But it is not I who should..."

"Please say no more!" Huitzitzilin shifted in the chair and smacked her lips, also demonstrating her feelings. "I have more to tell for your chronicle." She appeared to have forgotten about her hatred for Baltazar, as well as sin and punishment. She stared at Benito, waiting for him to produce his writing materials. Although she saw him hesitating, she prepared to continue with her story anyway.

The monk felt uncertain of going on because of the change in her. He felt that something was missing: a link to connect the intensity of the day before and her present relaxed air. He turned to gaze first at the fountain, then at the flowers; he was taking time to find an answer. When he returned his attention to Huitzitzilin, she had begun to speak, so he reached for quill and paper.

"When it was realized that Baltazar was missing, Captain Cortés launched a search for him. No matter where they looked or how many slaves were flogged or punished, Cortés was unable to discover anything leading to Baltazar's disappearance. Cortés, after a time, was forced to admit that it was futile to continue the investigation. Baltazar's wife returned to Spain along with most of her possessions, and their land went back to the king of Spain. We, the slaves and servants, were indentured to Captain Cortés.

"Tenochtitlan continued its transformation, so much so that it was now beyond our recognition. Captain Cortés prospered and his possessions grew. His household also expanded not only with new servants and slaves brought from other places, but from the birth of babies, most of them fathered by Spanish soldiers.

"I was placed in the scullery and laundry. Very little crossed my thoughts during those years, except that from time to time I would recall my childhood and young womanhood. Often, thoughts of my two boys, the ones who had been mine for a short while, filled my head. At other times I remembered Paloma, and in my mind I could see her growing into womanhood. I imagined her slender body, her breasts filling, her face radiant with the light of youth and laughter.

"These thoughts brought me a measure of consolation in the loneliness that clung to me. My life knew no joy, because my heart had dried up and because I was surrounded by unhappy, bitter people. So it was that one year followed the next. There was one exception: the year Captain Cortés returned to the land of his birth. He took many of us with him, as well as artifacts of gold and silver and gems."

"You've been to Spain?" Benito's face lit with surprise and admiration, realizing that here was yet another side to the woman that he had not imagined.

"Yes."

"Where? What city? Did you go to Seville?"

"My, my, young priest. Give me a moment to answer your questions with one response. Captain Cortés took us to where the king of Spain awaited him. We went to the city you call Barcelona."

Father Benito gazed at Huitzitzilin. Awe was stamped on his face. When he returned to writing, he did it as rapidly as possible, because he sensed that she had witnessed an historical moment in Cortés' life, as well as that of Spain. He also felt certain that his chronicle would contain yet another different and unrecorded incident.

"It was not a happy experience for Captain Cortés, because he was disdained at court when he proclaimed that he and a handful of soldiers had conquered the kingdom of the Mexicas. No one believed that it happened that way. No one was interested. Everyone was bored with him and with what he had to tell. I didn't feel compassion for him because I was convinced that he was paying for his many cruelties towards us, especially the torture and execution of Cuauhtémoc."

Benito squinted, trying to remember the documents he had studied regarding that encounter between the conqueror of Mexico and the king's incredulous courtiers. Those papers attested to the fact that Cortés had indeed been jeered. Benito even recalled several letters that accused the captain of arrogance and exaggeration. He had thought that it was untrue, and that those documents had been circulated only to create a false impression of how the captain was really perceived. Huitzitzilin's words, however, provided evidence of Cortés' humiliation in Spain.

"The experience was sadder for me than for the captain because it was then that I encountered my daughter Paloma. She was lovely, and I knew it was my daughter because she looked as I had when I was fifteen years of age. The only difference was her color, which was white.

But I soon discovered that her loveliness did not go deeper than her skin.

"When we were paraded for the benefit of those people, it was Paloma who outdid herself in mocking my deformity. By that time, I understood the language in which she spoke, and I had to bear the anguish she caused me when she ridiculed me, making the others laugh."

"Perhaps you were mistaken. How could you be certain that the young woman was your daughter?"

"She looked like me. Besides, later on I asked several of the servants about her name, and they told me that it was Doña Paloma Ovando. No. There was no doubt."

Father Benito put down the quill as he reconstructed the scene that Huitzitzilin had described. He was struck by the irony of a daughter scoffing her mother. What if Paloma had known the truth? He pursed his lips as he wondered how many people now living in Spain were the offspring of a man or a woman native to this land and yet had no notion of their ancestry. Benito pitied those people.

"You look saddened by my words."

Benito was jarred from his thoughts. "Yes. I'm sad to think that you were insulted by your daughter."

"But she didn't know who I was."

"Still, she should not have been so cruel with anyone, don't you agree?"

"Yes. It happened, nevertheless."

Huitzitzilin was quiet for a while; then she went on speaking. "Last night I had a dream. Would you like to hear it?"

Father Benito cocked his head and nodded in affirmation because he wanted to hear what such a woman would dream. He recalled his own sleepless night and wished that he had known that Huitzitzilin was dreaming during his wakeful hours.

"I dreamed that I was singing by a river bank. Around me were plants and flowers; there was fragrance in the air and snow on the peaks of the volcanoes. As I sang I saw that those whom I have loved, and who have died, surrounded me. Close to me was Zintle and my sons; even my mother and father approached me. There also were the nurses who had cared for me when I was a child, as well the girls who had been my playmates and even the midwife who had interpreted my future and given me my name.

"But my dream was strange because all of us were of the same age; there were no children and no elders, only young people. Even I had recovered my youth. My scars were gone and my eyes glowed with the fire and joy they had possessed before my mutilation. We all smiled as we had before our world ended, and we asked one another where we had been and to what lands we had traveled. Then I awoke."

Father Benito was staring at his hands as he listened to Huitzitzilin. When she stopped speaking, he looked at her questioningly.

"I have no more to tell you. Nothing has happened to me since my return from your land, except witnessing the transformation of our kingdom. I have watched as our buildings perished in the wake of yours, as our religion disappeared under the shadow of yours, and as the color of our skin became faded with the mixture of our blood with that of your race.

"All that I have left now are the memories of how my people were and of the greatness of Tenochtitlan. When I stroll the cloisters of this convent, I often converse with my dear ones, telling them of these sentiments. Surely you must have seen them during your visits?"

"I have seen you speaking, Señora."

"Have you seen them?"

"No, I haven't."

"They see you."

Benito's eyes narrowed to a slit as they scanned Huitzitzilin's face. Was she mocking him, trying to make him feel foolish again? She had done that several times since he began visiting her.

"I know that spirits exist, but I don't believe we can see them with our eyes that are mere flesh."

"That's because you don't try."

Father Benito decided not to respond, because he felt incapable of refuting what she had to say. He knew that Huitzitzilin was sincere in asserting contact with the spirits of her past life, and he did not want to contradict her.

"Many times when I walk arm in arm with Zintle through the shadows of the garden, we chat, recalling our childhood. Sometimes our teachers also join us, as does Father Motolinía. You might say that they are phantoms created by my memory, but I assure you that they are not. They are the spirits of those who loved me and who keep me company to this day."

"Our Lord Jesus Christ commands the spirits of us all."

Benito regretted the platitude as soon as the words left his lips, but it was too late because Huitzitzilin reacted to what he had said. Her expression told him that she had understood, but that she dissented.

"Our spirits will never be commanded by your young God."

"Please don't speak that way! You know that it is blasphemy!" Benito felt his hands begin to sweat. He thought of what Father Anselmo and the other monks would determine if they suspected that he was in conversation with one who spoke with such irreverence. Huitzitzilin stared at him in silence.

"Señora, now that we are nearing the end of our conversations, I implore you to recognize that the God of good has triumphed in this land."

"He was expelled from these parts generations ago."

"What!"

Benito realized that he and the woman were again on the verge of an argument. This bewildered him because he had thought that they had finally reached the point of understanding and respect. Huitzitzilin discerned the look on his face and interrupted what he was about to say.

"I'm speaking of Quetzalcóatl, the god of good. He was cast out of Anahuac by the forces of Huitzilipochtli and his gnome brother, Tezcatlipoca."

The monk was stumped. He saw that the woman still believed in the idols. Why had she not said this at the beginning when he might have understood that she was as yet unconverted? Her heresy filled him with frustration. He felt that he had wasted his time, because he saw that she still clung to the ancient tenets of her people. He got to his feet determined to walk out on her.

"No, young priest. Sit and listen to me. You have been sent to hear my words and to write them for those who will soon fill this land."

Father Benito responded to the grip of her hand on his forearm and returned to the chair. But he tried to show by his expression that he disapproved of the topic on which she was speaking.

"In their rage and anger at having lost their grasp of the Mexica, those two gods stalk our land to this day, and they will do so until the end of time. They await the god of good at every turn, in all places, prepared to provoke war."

Benito lowered his head. He wanted to respond to the woman's words with affirmations of Jesus and redemption and paradise and happiness, but he knew that at that moment they were trite, empty words that would fall flat the moment they crossed his lips. He kept quiet.

"As I told you, it was Moctezuma who saw the truth. The Mexica betrayed the god of good, and as a consequence they were crushed. Huitzilipochtli and his brother were not destroyed, however. They will roam this land of volcanoes and pyramids to the end of time."

Father Benito stood to leave. "I'll return tomorrow."

"What for? I have nothing more to tell."

He looked at Huitzitzilin as if for the first time. "I'll return tomorrow."

Chapter
XXIII

"She passed away during her sleep, but I don't think there was pain. She was old, and very fatigued."

The next morning, Father Benito stood listening to the nun who opened the convent doors. His mind scrambled, attempting to deal with the suddenness of Huitzitzilin's death. He was shocked. He kept still for a long while until the nun cleared her throat, letting him know that she was there.

"Step into the chapel. We're preparing her for burial." The nun began to move away from Benito, then stopped and looked at him. "She was very old, Father."

"Why haven't you notified the monastery?"

"We have. You probably crossed paths with our messenger."

"I see. I'll be along in a few minutes."

Instead of heading for the chapel, Benito entered the cloister and walked to the place where he and Huitzitzilin had sat the day before. He looked around at the flowers and the fountain. Nothing had changed. Then he sat on the usual chair, put his face in his cupped hands and remained there thinking for a long time.

The monk was struggling with the irrevocability of Huitzitzilin's death, as well as with his own intense disappointment. He had wanted to speak more with her, to listen to her thoughts on what she had said the day before. Now it was too late, and her voice saying that she had nothing more to say came back to him. After a while he was filled with a desire to see her, so he went to the chapel.

When Father Benito entered the small chapel, he found himself engulfed by the muted voices of nuns reciting prayers for the dead. The air was filled with the odor of incense, and the only light was that of candles. He saw that Huitzitzilin's body was on a bier in the center of the church; at each corner were ornately sculpted candelabra. Bunches of white flowers were clustered around the coffin. When Benito got close to her, he saw that her expression was peaceful. Her face, as he had thought many times, was that of a bird: small, beaked, alert. He could imagine, more than ever, that she had been beautiful when she was young.

As he stood by Huitzitzilin's side, the monk was touched by her spirit. He wondered if he returned to the cloister garden, to its shadows, would he be able to see her strolling with the people she had loved. The thought moved him to prayer, not one for a soul in purgatory, but for one in paradise: her paradise.

After a while, Benito left the chapel and went back to the cloister. He strolled for a time, then stopped to stand in a shaft of sunlight, listening to the water cascading from the fountain. He knew Huitzitzilin and her spirits were present, but he could not see them. Closing his eyes, he strained against the dullness of his own spirit that was blind and incapable of perceiving.

As he stood, eyes shut and face uplifted toward the sun, the monk slowly began to sense a humming sound. It was a lilting melody rising first from the earth beneath his feet, then from the stone walls of the convent, then from as far away as the volcanoes. The sensation grew within him until he realized that it was a song that he was feeling, although he could not hear it. He opened his eyes and retraced his steps through the cloister until he was out of the convent.

Father Benito walked for a long time as he headed for the heart of the city. He was drawn by a powerful desire to go to the center of what had been Huitzitzilin's world. When fatigue overcame him, he asked a man if he would allow him to ride on his cart. It took another long while before Benito got off the wagon and began to climb the hill.

The Mexicas called the mound Tepeyac, a place revered by them as the temple of the goddess of life. The Christians now honored it as the shrine of the Virgin of Guadalupe. On that elevated site, the monk sat in meditation. He felt that Huitzitzilin's spirit was again present. It was here, he recalled, that her marriage preparations had begun, and so had her story.

He gazed to the east and saw the outline of the volcanoes; he was grateful that something was still intact. Then he turned to the west, looking toward Tlaltelolco, Cuauhtémoc's kingdom and the site of the last battle for Tenochtitlan. There Benito made out the towering spires of the church of Santiago of Compostela; around it the rubble of destroyed pyramids and temples was still visible.

Huitzitzilin had often spoken of the silence that swept off the volcanoes to permeate Tenochtitlan. He listened and heard that silence. He knew that beneath, the city teemed with noisy bustle, but on Tepeyac the silence of the Mexicas still prevailed.

Her words, spoken the day before, foreseeing the conflict between the god of good and the gods of evil, resounded again, and they began to take shape and meaning for the priest. He now saw that he had resisted her because he misunderstood her words, and that he had thought that they were an assault on his religion. Looking down at the city that had been the mirror of Huitzitzilin's world, the monk regretted his angry response and rude departure.

"Will you forgive me?"

Unexpectedly, Huitzitzilin's words rang out as strong and clear as when she had sat beside him. Benito was startled, and his body stiffened. His eyes shifted from one side to the other searching for her, but there was nothing. Her spirit remained hidden from his eyesight.

Then her voice came to him again. *"Will you forgive me?"* This time the meaning of her words perplexed him even more than when he could see her. Why had she insisted on his forgiveness despite the affirmation that God had granted her pardon? Benito pondered the question, turning it over in his mind for a long time, until he realized that these words were at the heart of Huitzitzilin's story. His mind went deeper into his spirit until it became clear to him that it was not absolution or even mercy that she had expected of him, but understanding of her life, of her people, and of their beliefs. He saw, too, that for an unforeseen reason he had been chosen to record that life, to see it through her eyes in its wholeness and not in fragments.

The monk sighed as the silence wrapped itself around him, and he abandoned himself to his thoughts. He stayed on that high place for hours, meditating on Huitzitzilin's story, and it was only then that he felt a sudden rush of sadness. Dejection clung to him until he understood that she was now with those people who had been part of her life, those who had seen the world as she had seen it, those who had lived as she had lived. The priest then remembered Huitzitzilin's dream, where she had met her spirits on the bank of a river, and his sorrow lessened.

It was dark by the time Father Benito strode down Tepeyac and headed for the monastery. As he walked, Huitzitzilin's voice reverberated over and again. He made his way through the darkened city, wondering what could fill the emptiness created by her absence. His question was answered when he reminded himself that he had captured her words on paper and that her song would live on in Anahuac forever.